MURMUR

'With a masterful control that is surely almost a kind of
tenderness, Will Eaves brings Alan Turing close, looking
beyond logic and error to the greatest complexity of all –
compassion. Here is the aching loneliness of both human
indignity and dignity, despair and courage. *Murmur* is
penetrating, principled, profoundly moving. – Anne Michaels

'[*Murmur*] has achieved the holy grail of modern prose:
conveying consciousness . . . Even if it were merely another
tale about a courageous man or woman overcoming the odds
and discovering the fruits of love, nature and memory, it would
still be a very original handling. In taking those themes and
weaving them with our anxieties about the future, it is among
the first and best of its kind.' – Oscar Yuill, *Review 31*

'*Murmur* is a profound meditation on what machine consciousness might mean, the implications of AI, where it will all lead.
It's one of the big stories of our time, though no one else has
treated it with such depth and originality.' – Peter Blegvad

also by Will Eaves

FICTION

The Oversight
Nothing to Be Afraid Of
This Is Paradise
The Absent Therapist

POETRY

Sound Houses
The Inevitable Gift Shop

Will Eaves

MURMUR

 editions

First published in 2018
by CB editions
146 Percy Road London W12 9QL
www.cbeditions.com

Fourth impression April 2019

Printed in England by ImprintDigital, Exeter

ISBN 978–1–909585–26–3

He roves not like a runagate through all the world abroad;
This country hereabout (the which is large) is his abode.
He doth not, like a number of these common wooers, cast
His love to everyone he sees. Thou art the first and last
That ever he set mind upon. Alonely unto thee
He vows himself as long as life doth last. Moreover he
Is youthful and with beauty sheen endued by nature's gift,
And aptly into any shape his person he can shift.
Thou canst not bid him be the thing, though all things thou
    shouldst name,
But that he fitly and with ease will straight become the same.
Besides all this, in all one thing both twain of you delight,
And of the fruits that you love best the firstlings are his right,
And gladly he receives thy gifts. But neither covets he
Thy apples, plums, nor other fruits new gathered from the tree,
Nor yet the herbs of pleasant scent that in thy gardens be,
Nor any other kind of thing in all the world, but thee.

    – Ovid, *Metamorphoses*, Book XIV, trans. Arthur Golding

The world is given but once. Nothing is reflected.

    – Erwin Schrödinger, 'Mind and Matter' (1956)

PART ONE

JOURNAL

Murmur

Fear of homosexuals is never far from the surface. The few people who have supported me after my conviction must be very strong-minded. I do not think most people are equipped to associate with pariahs. They have a shadowy sense of how frail they themselves would be in the face of institutional opposition and stigmatisation, how utterly cast down if they lost their jobs, if people they knew stopped serving them in shops or looked past them in the street. It is not hatred that turns the majority against the minority, but intuitive shame.

★

Do I need to set down the circumstances? The results are in the papers, and once again I am disinclined to 'show my working'. It is strangely more instructive, for me, to imagine other conditions, other lives. But here they are, so that my friends, when they come to these few thoughts, may do likewise.

I had just finished a paper and decided to award myself a pick-up. I met the boy, Cyril, on the fairground. He seemed undernourished and shifty but not unengaging; living, he said, in a hostel, working casually. I bought him pie and chips on the grounds and invited him home for the weekend. He didn't turn up, so I went back to Brooker's, waited for the fair to close that night, and took him home soon after. He was not unintelligent, I found — he'd liked the boys' camp in the war, did some arithmetic there, and knew about *Mathematical Recreations*. Cyril was, I'd say, the product of natural sensitivity, working-class starvation and nervous debility. He wouldn't kiss. We treated ourselves to baths and listened to the late repeat of the *Brains Trust* programme on learning machines, with Julius Trentham opining, not implausibly in my view, that the human ability to learn is determined by 'appetites, desires, drives, instincts' and that a learning machine would require 'something corresponding to a set of appetites'. And I said something like, 'You see, what I find interesting about that is Julius's suggestion that all these feelings and appetites, as he calls them, are causal, and programmable. Even these things, which we're so sure, so instinctively certain, must be the preserve of freely choosing and desiring humans, may be isolated. They can be caused, and they have a cause.' And Cyril was fascinated. He was listening and nodding. I felt so happy and so peculiarly awful. We went to bed and in the morning I unthinkingly offered him some money. He was offended and left in a mood. I then discovered £3 missing from my wallet — he could have taken it at any time, I put nothing away — and I wrote to him at the hostel, calling things off. He turned up on the doorstep the next day, very indignant, making obscure threats which I did not take seriously. He mentioned an unlikely-sounding suit-hire debt, for £3 of course, and some other outstanding sums and then ended up asking for another £7, which I reluctantly gave him.

A week later, I returned home from the university to find my house broken into, not much taken, £10 from a drawer, some silver plate. I reported the break-in. The police came to the house and fingerprinted it. I also consulted a solicitor in confidence about the possibility of Cyril blackmailing me, and on his advice again wrote to the boy, breaking things off. Cyril subsequently appeared at my house, as before, and this time the threats were not obscure but explicit: he would go to the police and it would come out about the 'Professor' and his chums. We had a row, I mentioned the burglary, and he calmed down and kissed me for the first time, and said that he knew who might have done it – his mate from the navy. He admitted having boasted of his friendship with me and I was foolishly flattered. Cyril stayed the night and I went to the police station in the morning with some information about the likely culprit and a rather shoddy story about how I'd come by it. The fingerprints, meanwhile, clearly identified Cyril's naval friend, who already had a criminal record and needed little prompting to blab about Cyril's 'business' with me.

The King died in the early hours of the day on which two very kind police officers paid me a visit. Seven weeks after my arrest, I was found guilty of gross indecency with a male person and sentenced to receive a course of organo-therapy – hormone injections – to be delivered at the Royal Infirmary. The physical effects of those injections have been marked. Almost at once I began dreaming. I do not think deeply about Cyril, it turns out, but about others I think as deeply as anyone can.

★

Things seem to be sadly lost, put to bed, left on top of golden summits in the past, trailing away until we see what the lines of event and memory have traced: a plane. A loop that encloses all loss, has no beginning and no end.

★

I wonder about the coming together of events and people that have produced my crisis. If I were to find a mathematical or topological analogy, I suppose that it would be 'tessellation' – where the contours of one form fit perfectly the contours of another. If I had not finished the paper on morphogenesis when I did, I should not have ventured out in search of a reward. If had not had the upbringing I did have, I should not have thought of sexual relations as a candidate for 'reward'. The very interesting Mr Escher, whose prints have finally awoken my fellow mathematicians to the possibility of an aesthetics of undecidability, has called this coming together the 'regular division of the plane', but it is a little more than that, because it is a division that entails change. The world is not atomistic or random but made of forms that interlock and are always interlocking, like the elderly couple in Ovid who become trees. Time is the plane that reveals this interlocking, though time is not discrete. You cannot pin it down. Very often you cannot see the point at which things start to come together, the point at which cause generates effect, and this is a variant of the measurement problem. It must also be akin to asking at what point we begin to lose

6

consciousness when we are given an anaesthetic, or at what point unconscious material becomes conscious. Where does one cross over into the other? If the tessellation of forms is perfect, do they divide? Or are they one?

★

In the third century of the Roman occupation, people buried money for safekeeping, so wary were they of political instability and the possibility of tribal insurrection. Favourite burial places were woodlands, the natural shrines of outcrops and waterfalls; springs and high ground. I read of this in Jacquetta Hawkes's invaluable history of these islands. The Romans borrowed the traditions of the late Iron Age natives and burying wealth became not merely a rite of propitiation but an act of generosity, not a symbol of something but a self-contained reality, as important as the giving of oneself to the day, every day. Into the ground they went – bags of coins, silver denarii, gold solidi, pots of chaff, figurines of fauns and satyrs, phalluses, antlers, votive objects, brooches, spearheads, bridle rings, weapons and shields, and cauldrons of course. The cradle of the feast. It is difficult, after the cataclysm, to retrieve one's thinking at the time, but when war was declared I, too, amassed my savings, or a goodly chunk of them, and bought two silver ingots and buried them. I did not find them again. I have them not, and yet I believe that they still exist somewhere and that they are of value. The evidence is lacking and I appear not to be interested in the evidence after all: my belief is that I have lost something of value. If only we could believe we were just carbon and water, we could leave life behind very phlegmatically, but belief gets in the way. Because: what is belief?

★

Living on your own makes you more tolerant of people who say strange things. I met a dog-walker on the common recently who greeted me as I rounded the bandstand as if I were a close friend returning to her side after a trip to the toilet. She looked over the misty grass and said casually, 'This is where I scattered my father's ashes.' I suppose she was in some sort of pain. Pain is the invisible companion. At the fairground, where I met Cyril, there were the remains of freaks – strong men and a boxing booth with a poor giant of a man soaking up the most dreadful punishment, but also a woman with hyperextended limbs. Freaks live in pain, as do most sporting types and ballet dancers. So much of real life is invisible.

★

These are notes to pass the time, because I am in a certain amount of discomfort. I suppose it is fear, and keeping a partial journal distracts me. But I am also drawn to the pulse of that fear, a beat, an elevated heart rate – and something more than that, which comes through the thinking and is a sort of rhythmic description of my state of mind, like someone speaking quickly and urgently on the other side of a door.

I know that Pythagoras is said to have delivered his lectures from behind a screen. The separation of a voice from its origin gave him a wonder-inducing authority, apparently. Perhaps he was shy. Or ugly. Anyway, I've never had this experience before. This morning I could hear the inner murmuring accompanying trivial actions: 'I'm up early, it's dark outside, the path I laid haphazardly with my own hands is now a frosted curve. I put some crumbs down for the blackbird singing on my neighbour's chimney pot. Beyond my garden gate a road, beyond that fields speeding away towards the tree-lined hills and crocus light. I wait beside a bare rowan, its berries taken by the blackbird and her brood, the wood pigeons and jays.' And then again, moments later, when I caught myself looking back at the garden through the doorway: 'He passes through the silent streets, across wet roofs and closed faces, deserted parks. He moves among the trees and waiting fairground furniture.'

The error is supposed to be 'looking back', isn't it? Poor Orpheus, etc.

Of course, it has occurred to me that the balance of my mind is disturbed, just as it has occurred to me that I am reckoning with a deliberate retreat from the world, a passing out of sight into, well, invisibility. What lesson might that passage have for me? It is an extension of my preference for anonymity, I suppose. It is commonly said, or felt if it is not said, that people respect others of importance who have achieved things or held office; but it is a curious fact that self-respect is often found to exist in inverse proportion to public status. It has learned to pass nights alone. It does not seek approval because it knows that estimation has nothing to do with achievement.

★

Though it is doubtless an impolitic thing for a material-ist to admit, I cannot help wondering if the real nature of mind is that it is unencompassable by mind, and whether that Godelian element of wonder – at something we know we have, but cannot enclose – may not be the chief criterion of consciousness.

★

There is a picture book in the Royal Infirmary waiting room. I think it is an attempt to improve me, or to give the sickly reasons to get well (art, culture, all of it waiting to be appreciated!) should medicine struggle to oblige. It contains a reproduction of Poussin's *The Triumph of David*. I was struck by the painting, which I did not know. In particular I was struck by the fact that the young Israelite and the waxy outsized head of Goliath, the slain Philistine, wore similar expressions. They seemed sad, as if they had glimpsed, beyond the immediate joy and horror, echoes of the act in history – its wave-like propagation of revenge.

★

A gardener, today, laying out the common beds for the council: 'A whole mob of crows died in the meadow a few years ago. They did autopsies, because it was such an unusual event. But they died of old age. They were about seventeen.' Christopher's age.

★

That life has arisen on this planet might be regarded as a matter for amazement. That it should arise on many others would be, on the face of it, if true, even more amazing. The repeated escape from, as Schrödinger puts it, 'atomic chaos' would be not just one sense-defying statistical fluctuation but a whole series of them. It would be like throwing handfuls of sand into the wind and finding, when the grains are settled, tiny replicas of the Taj Mahal, St Paul's Cathedral and the temple complex of Angkor Wat upon the ground. It would be very lovely, but unlikely. Luckily for us, however, the statistical system of the universe has about it a marvellous impurity, which is that it functions also as a dynamical system or mechanism for the maintenance and reproduction of order over long stretches of time. Or, to be disappointingly precise, the prolonged illusion of order, because the statistics of thermal disorder are all still there in the background and, like suspicious tax officers, they will get to us in the end. The art of living then, on this view, is simply that of defying them for as long as possible, until equilibrium, which isn't as nice as it sounds, is restored.

★

The alarming truth is that you can't grasp your own condition, though you suspect that something is wrong. You see yourself on the edge of a black hole, or a bowl, or a cauldron, whereas, in reality, you have disappeared down inside it.

★

You know your social life is in trouble when you spend the evening reading an article on puzzles called 'Recreational Topology'. I don't have any kind of social life. It's topologically invariant under many deformations, you might say, although probably only someone without a social life would bother to say that.

★

The other part of my rehabilitation, or punishment, or both, consists of fortnightly meetings with a psychoanalyst, Dr Anthony Stallbrook. I have approached this with circumspection. I find, however, that it is not as I had been led to expect. He is a most sympathetic, comfortably tiny person with fuzz around the ears and a pate that shines like a lamp in his study and lights the way to two armchairs. No couch. We chat. We go for walks and trips. We are not supposed to go for walks and trips, but then he does not believe in his assignment, that homosexuals require any rehabilitation, or that there is time to be lost where friendship is concerned. Neither does his wife. We are planning a trip to Brighton. Our sessions together founder somewhat on the reef of his presuppositions: I have searched my conscience for repressed feelings and find none. I loved Christopher and had fantasised about a future that involved us living and working together. He took me seriously. I am quite sure that I never fooled myself into believing that he felt intimately about me as I felt about him. His friendship would have been enough. My fantasies were outrageously Platonic, and I have never stopped loving him. At the same time, I am haunted by his presence, molecular, gaseous, call it what you will – and the nearness of his voice and person, on the lip of conscious experience, is a constant anxiety made worse by my own changes. He is as near to me as I am near to the person I used to be, and both persons are irretrievable.

Dr Stallbrook often asks me how I feel. I reply that I do not know. How *does* one feel? It is one of the imponderables. I am better equipped to say *what* it is that I feel, and that is mysterious enough. For I feel that I am a man stripped of manhood, a being but not a body. Like the Invisible Man, I put on clothes to give myself a stable form. I'm at some point of disclosure between the real and the abstract – changing and shifting, trying to stay close to the transformation, not to flee it. I have the conviction that I am now something like x – a variable. We discuss dreams, and in the course of these discussions I have come to see dream figures as other sets of variables. How else should one account for the odd conviction we have in dreams that the strangers we encounter are 'really' people we know?

What gets us from one expression of the variable to another?

There is a leap from the inorganic to the organic. There is a leap from one valency to another, and there is a leap from one person's thought to the thought of others. The world is full of discrete motes, probabilistic states, and gaps. Only a wave can take us from one to the other; or a force or flow; or perhaps a field. When I look in the mirror, I think, thrice, 'Is it me? Is it not me? Is it not me, yet?'

Dr Stallbrook encourages me to write. It is like making a will, he says – eminently sensible. If you've signed your papers and made a will, you know there will be an end. You have already witnessed it, so to speak. And people who make this definite accommodation with their end, with the prospect of death – who get it in writing – live longer. He says this with a matter-of-factness I can't help liking.

*

Julius and others belabour me with questions about thinking machines and the parallels between chains of neurons in the brain and the relationship of the controlling mechanism to output and feedback in digital computers. I want fair play for the computer, of course. I feel, as he does, that 'understanding' in a machine is a function of the relationship between its rules. Recursion may turn out to be reflection in both the optical and the philosophical senses of the word.

Who knows what machines may end up 'thinking'? But I am privately sceptical of too wide an application of the personifying tendency. One knows oneself to be aware and infers from others – from behaviour, yes, but also from the body or the instrument that produces the behaviour – that they are similarly cognisant. One can't go on from there to supposing that awareness itself is necessary, however. Hasn't it struck most of us at one time or another that much of life is a pointless algorithm, an evolutionary process without an interpreter. On a smaller scale, too, a process such as simple addition has human 'meaning' only because I am there to observe it and call it 'addition'. And yet it certainly happens. Perhaps the larger process, too, is unmeaningful. If life works, it works. The character of physical law as it extends to biological material is that it should underpin the way cells and systems operate, and that is all.

That sounds pleasingly final, but it won't do. I know that. Things don't always add up. I can tell you that it is asymmetrical motion at the molecular level that picks out an axis for patterned development in a sphere of cells – that turns a sphere into an embryo – but I cannot satisfy the person who goes on asking 'why?' That person is the halfwit in a public lecture. That person is a child. And that person is also me. The Church says: 'People come in search of meaning, and to have their fears and anxieties allayed.' But to think you can be finally satisfied on these points, or to imagine you can satisfy others, is the source of the misgiving.

★

I have this strange idea. Christopher left school without saying goodbye. His parents came to pick him up and I saw them get in the Daimler. I was in the upper gallery, working on some diagonals. I looked askance, through the window, and there they were, thanking the Headmaster, hurrying away. I heard no more from Christopher or his mother, with whom I imagined myself friendly, until the notice of his death. I had not known he was consumptive. He had cold hands.

This is the idea. We, Chris and I, were reprimanded for scrumping apples from the trees that overhung the chaplain's garden. They belonged to Fowle's fruiterers. We were punished and interviewed separately. I think he was told to avoid me. I think he was told no good could come of our friendship, because of what I am, or rather, because of what, then, it was suggested I would become. I am not effeminate, but I am mannered. I am a homosexual, and I suppose that much was clear to the masters. In particular, I think it was impressed on Chris that some polluting disaster would befall *me*, and if only he had asked 'why?', my future ghost might have told him.

★

Dr Stallbrook makes many notes as we go along, talking and arguing, and it has crossed my mind that patients of different stripes must react differently to this. I confess I find it irritating. I do not like being 'marked', or having my papers tampered with editorially, or submitting to a 'clinical' opinion I am not in a position to check. (I was displeased when I found out that I had been circumcised.) And if his notes are, as he claims, 'for his eyes only', then they are unfalsifiable. They may well proceed from a psychoanalytic theory. But how is the theory being tested or controlled? How can it be said to be scientific? He is unflappable, of course. It is not that kind of theory, he says; it is, rather, *theoria*, from the Greek, meaning 'contemplation'. The look of point-missingly clever satisfaction on his face! Anyway, he is not telling the truth. I am a criminal. He is writing reports and sending them off.

The whole premiss is childish, like the schoolboy who covers his work with his elbow to prevent his neighbour cheating. I told him this.

'I'm really not trying to hide anything, Alec,' he laughed. 'I just don't think you'd benefit from reading my notes. My job is to help you *encounter yourself.*'

I replied, in a bit of a torrent: 'Balls. This is passing the buck. This is what my father saw in India all the time – Europeans waving their hands and saying, "But the unrest is *native* and has nothing to do with us." You are not an impartial observer, Dr Stallbrook. The observer is a partic-ipant, as the great revolution in quantum physics has taught us. Consider now that I am the set of notes that *you* wish to read. I might as well ask: how are you to benefit from reading me? Shall we condemn ourselves to solipsism? The two sides of an equation must meet if they are to balance. You are dodging the issue. What you want is for me not to press too deeply, not to ask for things you cannot give, not to question your authority. And that is unfair.'

'What do you mean?'

At this point, I lost my temper. 'The assumption of sci-ence is that things are discoverable. Things that belong in problems of logic that are not in principle resolvable belong in a separate category. Things that do not admit of rational argument in another – God, for instance. But things that are just hidden, or powers that are reserved for no good reason because someone 'says so', are the work of the bloody devil! They are a cryptic burden to us all – '

I was half out of my chair, and sat back heavily, because I'd come upon one of my own restrictions and couldn't believe I'd hidden it so effectively from myself.

The Act constrains me, of course. Aspects of my working past are always to be concealed from Dr Stallbrook. With the result that I am confined to addressing my personal life – aspects of which are presumably concealed from me.

Noticing my discomfiture, Anthony asked me what I was thinking. He sounded very kind, and I wanted to equal him in cooperation. Whenever I have not been able to persuade someone, I have tried to cooperate. I take this view even in respect of my conviction. One should meet bad manners with good grace.

'I'm sorry,' I said. 'I respect a necessary authority. But I do not like dodges or masquerades. Puzzles, yes. Masquerades, no.'

'Is this a masquerade?'

'No.' And I was sullenly silent for a while, thinking distractedly and angrily that civilised England is a masquerade. The War Room is a masquerade when the real thing is far away. Psychoanalysts are doubtless persons of integrity, but persons of integrity may still be pawns. There is usually some rule governing our voluntary actions that we either do not know about or are unwilling to acknowledge – the motives of the companies that pay our salaries and ask us to do things, the real function of justice, and so on. 'No,' I continued, 'but this is nevertheless a *game* with prohibitions we are playing, and one in which you have the advantage.

Your opinion of me counts, whatever I say. If you were to decide that I constituted a danger to society, you could have me locked away in a mental institution. But I cannot affect what happens to you. And the further disadvantage to me is that there are things I simply cannot tell you, because I have given my word to others – others in authority – and even the confidences of our arrangement shall not tempt me, because a secret is a personal vow of custody. It cannot be handed over to someone else for safekeeping. And now you will think *I* am being unfair, and even obstructive.'

'No,' said Dr Stallbrook, carefully, 'that is not what I think.'

We brooded for a while, and the tension eased.

★

Also: just because something is discoverable doesn't mean one has any idea of how the discovering is to be done. One experiments, and sometimes there is a breakthrough and sometimes one has to admit defeat. How is one consciously to encounter one's subconscious? The gap is unbridgeable, it seems to me.

Love is a gap. I used to look at Chris while we were tinkering with chemicals and I'd carry on a conversation, adjusting retorts, making notes, apologising. Thinking all the while: this must be possible; clearly it is, for others manage it. But how?

★

Tolstoy's accounts of Borodino and Austerlitz show us what real war is like: no one knows what the orders are or who is winning. No one has any idea what to do. Soldiers are permitted to kill each other and are maddened, sooner or later, by the realisation that someone else, somewhere relatively comfortable, thinks this is the right thing for them to do. And we are not so far from that kind of chaos in everyday life, really. I walk down the street towards the Infirmary, every Wednesday, and I go in and wait and sit down and everyone is quite polite, and I am played with by the law and turned into a sexless person. The most extraordinary thing is done behind a nice white screen. And the nurse who injects me does it with a good will, because she has been told that it is her job. She doubtless thinks of herself as a freely choosing agent. She likes to think she does her job well, but at the same time she is *just doing her job*. (One hears this a lot.) That means she does not take ultimate responsibility for her actions, because those kinds of decisions are taken, or absorbed, by more powerful persons, like Tolstoy's generals, who know what they are doing. She sees no contradiction between this and her own intuitive sense of agency.

She goes home to her parents' house and has her tea. They have put up some new frieze wallpaper with a ribbon of classical-looking dancing figures where a picture rail might have been. It looks pretty and I wonder how often the family has looked at the actual figures in the frieze, copied from vases in the British Museum by some impish and bored designer. The figures are a) playing music, b) killing their enemies, and c) engaged in exotic but mechanical sexual relations.

We agree not to look. It is a simple but profound contract of the collective subconscious with the truth. If you speak the truth, or do something which indicates how human beings function, regardless of the law, regardless of moral superstition, then people will turn against you, and you must never underestimate how fearful and weak most people in a large body, like a government, or a university, or even an office, actually are. Once you have been isolated in this way, you can be dismissed.

★

I wish people who believe in God could believe in him a little less fervently – could see him as a metaphor for the boundedness of our physical existences and the problem of the mental, which is physical too, but perhaps in a way we don't understand.

★

'You're doing tremendously well!' or even 'You're looking well on it' means: 'Please don't tell me any more about your plight, but instead reassure me that I don't have to worry about this.' Similarly, hilariously, 'We know what it's like. We've just had the most awful trouble with . . .' means: 'We are not going to help you.'

But they are helping, my neighbours, and I am cruel. They want me to teach their son chess. He is a pleasant chap with no great aptitude (yet) for the game, or for calculation in general, and I suspect that he likes the barley water at the end of our lessons most of all. He stumbles over my name, and speaks inaudibly, which I find upsetting.

★

Doctors can be terribly self-important without realising it because they get to point and diagnose, and if they're point-ing at you then of course that means you're not pointing at them. Pointers are an odd lot. They want the triumphant power of clarifying something, of accusation, but they're also jealously private. They don't want to be pointed out themselves: it's a sort of nightmare for them, which leads to them pointing at others more and more often, more and more vehemently. I tend to do it when I get cross. It's an extremely unappealing habit born of heaven knows what guilt and insecurity. But I don't do it so much now – now that I've been pointed out once and for all, as it were. Perhaps I've realised I just *don't* feel guilty of this so-called crime. The whole thing is . . . pointless. It rather frees one up.

Stallbrook is at least intelligent. The endocrinologist at the Infirmary told me, 'These are conservative measures. The hormone is effective rather than strong. There shouldn't be side effects.' It is effective, but in a way that doesn't have effects.

★

I liked the Fun Fair and Festival Pleasure Gardens, but I love the old fairs more.

At the Festival there were approved attractions – the tree walk, the water chute, the grand vista, the Guinness Clock, and a marvellously eccentric children's railway, designed by the *Punch* cartoonist Mr Emett. This last innovation had a locomotive called Nellie, with an engine sandwiched between a pavilioned passenger car and, to the rear, a copper boiler surrounded by a wonky fence. Britain on the move! A weathervane sat on top of the boiler, and a whistle in the shape of a jug. Everything seemed thin and elegant, a series of wiry protrusions, like an undergraduate. The whistle itself adorned a chopped-off lamp post and a dovecote. It presented an unconscious picture of bomb damage and higgledy-piggledy reconstruction.

Oh, but it was lifeless! In the Hall of Mirrors, for example, I noticed an absence of the laughter one encounters on the seasonal fairground or in Blackpool or Brighton, on the pier. Instead one had the sense that, in looking at themselves all bent out of shape, people were being reminded of what was not quite right about their day out as whole, which was that the jollity felt forced, and polished up, and that the element of lawlessness that is so necessary to a carnival was missing.

As it happened, just up the road, Brooker's fair had come to the common, as it does every year, and that was a proper raffish fair of the old type, with stalls and toffee apples, and fish for prizes, and overcoated old ladies in the payboxes of the dodgems (and the gallopers and the chairoplanes) keeping an eye on the hordes, and gaff lads riding the waltzers, and duckboards underfoot (the common has marshy spots), and caravans, and lights everywhere, and yes, the fighting booth, with a few rather tragical-looking curiosities no longer called freaks but 'Wonders of the World'. In fifty years' time, you will have my machine in a booth, of course; or better yet my test, and instead of the sign outside the booth saying 'Are you a Man or a Mouse?' it will say 'Are you a Man or a Machine?' (And the answer will be: both.)

It is an erotic place, the fair. Everything about it – the mushrooming appearance, the concentration of energy, the scapegrace hilarity, the ambush and occupation of common land, the figures moving in the trees after the covers go on and the lights are out – bespeaks the mortal. This is your chance, it says. Take it!

He was wearing a very threadbare black suit, with a grubby white shirt.

The girls, away from their concerned mothers, were hanging about the novelty rides with the flashier gaffers, the ones with studded belts and rings on their fingers and satin cuffs on their shirtsleeves – the ones with sideburns and cowboy swagger. They are not handsome, these lads, and they're filthy dirty from all the putting up of rides and maintenance, but their attraction – to the girls – is their daring, the way they leap about the tracks, hitching rides on cars and leaping off again, and of course the fact that they do not have to be introduced to anyone.

But I preferred Cyril, who was dressed, as I say, in a suit, who seemed shy, and said 'Thank you, sir' in a soft deep voice when I handed over my money. He didn't quite belong with the other gaffers, which meant he was a new hire and not formerly known to the Brookers. And he had a moment's uncertainty – I caught his eye – when he counted out the change and saw that I knew what he was doing.

The double spin – the spin within a spin – of the waltzers prompted me to think about the n-body problem and waves of chemical concentration in a ring of cells, so I was happy to pay for another ride. Well, that wasn't the only reason. This time he gave me the right change and a smile. I took a risk and said: 'I'd like to know how that is done.' 'How what is?' he replied, frowning, and moved on to the next car. But I waved when I got off and his grin was a flash of mixed emotions.

I gave him lunch, which he wolfed down, and we talked. I don't think I expected him to respond to my weekend offer. Asking for things entails a loss of esteem, but he didn't absolutely say no and so I concluded he had been embarrassed rather than put off, and I went back a few days later and loitered.

Though these assignations do not last long, the moment invariably spreads out.

The first thing he did when we met in the trees, in a small bower of hawthorn, was to pick a spiny twig out of the way and thread it safely behind a larger branch moving in another direction. That meant he could then lay his head on my lapel and put his hands on my arms, as if he were bracing himself for something. The tender contract signed, we went about our business very efficiently – Cyril eagerly taking the woman's role, as men least willing to admit their taste mostly do – and the mood changed. The reward for competence is suspicion and, between men, a ruthless brio designed to break the bonds of troublesome affection. Luckily, I am not jealous. 'I want some more,' Cyril whispered to me. 'You can watch if you like.' So I did. He slipped from our shelter into the main clearing and soon found his way, turning jauntily as he walked – almost skipped – to another tree-fringed island where a group of men from the caravans took turns with him. One of them stuffed a handkerchief in his mouth. Cyril turned his head, all eyes, mouth filled up with dots, to look at me while this was going on, to see if I was still there, to see if I was shocked. I was fascinated, of course, and pleased he was enjoying himself, but concerned in a different way. His legs looked thin and white and unfinished with the trousers dropped about his shoes, like the bones of a more robust ancestor.

When the men were done, I went over and asked Cyril if he would like a bed for the night, and he was polite and gentle again, and said yes, that would be lovely. We listened to the radio, as I have said. He told me several of the riding masters went with lads and that it was one of the perks of the life. He said that there is usually one who becomes the 'dolly tub', a term Cyril did not like, and that sometimes it was very good and others it was too rough and a worry. He would not admit to prostitution and so I made the mistake with the money, which is perhaps why he stole from me. I think being a gaff was a source of pride.

These are, or were, the contributing circumstances. I view them unsentimentally. It is interesting that I do not consider their rehearsal to be a serious kind of thought. Underneath them run echoes and rills of a different order, however, the inner murmur, and these I take to be true thinking, determinate but concealed.

In the middle of the night, with his back to me, and his skin warm, he explained how the short-changing or 'tapping' was, after all, supposed to be done.

'The rich flat' — flats or flatties are trade, the punters — 'the rich flat hands me the money, say a ten-bob note for a half-shilling ride, and I take it to Queenie in the paybox. There's no fooling Queenie, because she can tell who's on the ride, how many, how much should be coming in, so I can't diddle her.' He paused to cough, and I felt his ribs. 'Not so hard!' He settled his head back into the pillow. 'So I collect the change, florins, bobs and sixpences, and go back to the customer, and I count it out from my left hand to my right so he can see it's right: "Two, four, five, six, seven, eight, nine, nine-and-six, and the ride makes ten." Now it's all in my right hand, in the palm, but as I tip the coins into the flat's hand, I squeeze my palm, like, to keep hold of a few coins. The ride is running up by this point, so the customer doesn't notice what has happened.' He swallowed. 'Or he shouldn't. It takes a bit of practice. Takes a bit of nerve. I saw you and thought, this one won't shop me. Bit old for me, but not bad.' I could sense his eyes opening in the dark. 'And that's how you do it.'

'I know the weight of the alloy,' I said. 'Two florins and five shillings and sixpence should weigh approximately one and nine-tenths of an ounce.'

'You didn't have to look?'

I said that I liked to trust people, which I do. Lying there, I seemed to float outside my body and look down at us both. The objective viewpoint. I could see him laughing into the pillow, his eyes going right through the wall into the ivy and the street.

PART TWO

LETTERS AND DREAMS

When the body dies, the 'mechanism' of the body holding the
spirit is gone and the spirit finds a new body sooner or later,
perhaps immediately. . . . The body provides something for the
spirit to look after and use.
– A. M. Turing, unpublished note

The Field of Endeavour

Dear June,

*No, the loneliness itself does not distress me, as I do not under-
stand what most people mean by it. There is my home life, itself
solitary, and then there is work. I cannot be cut off by the treatment,
because I am already cut off by inclination. It is a matter of choice. I
am not one for poetry ('Count me out on this one'!! Am I permitted
to quote myself?), but I did admire M. Baudelaire's poem about a
man and his inner life: 'Qui ne sait pas peupler sa solitude, ne sait
pas non plus être seul dans une foule affairée.' Well, that is me –
populously on my tod!*

*Work, too, is separate, a separation from the world almost, and
the more I do what principally defines me, the more I realise I'm not
meant to have ordinary relationships, which seem to me, when I look
at all the men and women in the department, so often unsuccessful
precisely because the contracted sharing of time and space undefines
couples, as individuals I mean. No more relaxed chat in the pub,
curfew at seven, the inlaws coming for the day. And though I'd
never say it aloud (but can to you, who understand), I can't help*

feeling that marriage by and large has the most deplorably erosive effect on one's ability to think.

The work suffers, and the person who needs his work becomes almost negligent of his suffering in that regard. (And then of course the community of science suffers, and that is the sort of community I do believe in.)

I asked Trentham (nostrils, galoshes, very tall) the other day if he wanted to talk about his 'field awareness' paper after hours and he practically flinched with embarrassment. 'The little man,' he said, 'has got the measles.'

It wasn't that, of course, or not just that. And I don't believe he thought I had any ulterior motive. He's quite the unsuspicious sort (and indeed not for me). His whole vitality just seemed to ebb away, the shoulders sagged and he loped off, red-eyed, head thrust forward in a parody of concentrated endeavour, as much as to say, 'I've made this pact and now I'm stuck with it.'

I've met his wife. She's very nice. They're both charming, of course they are. I do feel, though, that shared existence entails a loss of privacy, and privacy, mental solitude at any rate, is absolutely essential, as you know.

The ones that work, the marriages, are based on such tolerance, such frank distance, that one is bound to ask the point of them in the first place. The world's opinion, I suppose, and maybe that's a good enough reason.

I've made myself another tidy paradox, haven't I? I'm all but saying, with my love of the solitary virtue, that I'm the perfect candidate for some discreet entanglement – but that would never do. Because although I do yearn for friends, for companionship, and in my own way for you, my dear June, very much, I do also feel that the business of yearning, for me, is a sort of proof of liberty – the imagining of what I want mustn't be interrupted, or the fancy fleeth.

It's peculiar. It's something, like the working out of a particular problem, I can do only on my own — like dreaming. Speaking of which, yes, I am still beset by the man in the mirror. He is with me nightly, daily. My doctor is fascinated, naturally, and wants to know everything. But there is very little I can tell him, and less he would understand. The impression is vivid while I am waking — he is a man, I think, and a man in distress, a prisoner of some description? — and lasts about as long as it takes for me to get to the desk, where I begin to write, and then . . .

Love to you,

A.

★

Before it's light, the first planes make their last approach, a noise like children blowing across milk bottles. The sound dips with the wind. Passengers, freight, the half-awake break through the clouds and settle on the ground. An open-eyed man hears these bottle-blowers from his bed, where he has passed the night wondering, recovering, steeling himself to wait out various embassies of doubt: *You may struggle to speak, you may not know that you can speak or have spoken. It will be difficult in different ways, when you are with others, when you're alone. Try to conserve your energy.*

Which he has done, letting the dark merely be dark, the curtain rail merely a row of hooks and not a file of iron imps hauling up canvases. Sometimes it seems as if the night has been one long held breath, until the planes arrive, the heating starts, and water flares and prickles in the pipes.

The reassuring forms emerge, the shelves of books, the desk, the built-in cupboard and the bed, his hands holding a grey herringbone blanket holed by moths. A small white label in one corner of the blanket reads 'Alec'. (The surname is obscured.) He gets up, wanders over to the desk and scribbles with the shivery sense that being up so early ought to give him an advantage – clarity. Except the world is up at the same time. Its silent armies stand revealed. His pen hovers. He wants to work, and working is at first invigorating and then too tiring. He hasn't yet remembered how to use the computer. It isn't him holding the pen. He sees the page moving beneath his nib in strokes and curves that form letters. The trail of ink is indecipherable. He feels so sick and out of breath; he nods his head.

Sleep comes as, miles away, the passengers step off the plane. They leave behind such quantities of rubbish – peanuts scattered over Ararat, coffee poured down the Rhine. What are they for, these airport trolleys with the orange beacons, nuzzling the belly of the plane? Inside the airport building, everyone shuffles. A man clears immigration with a yawn. The next couple are moved from queue to booth to closed office, where after several hours they learn that they will be deported and accept the bad news with surprising grace. The office windows frame a view of wet ground that's unreachable, less true than a recalled image of bare toes, sun and a warm puddle, foothills, goats. The city and the London life that might have been are meaningless as torchbeams aimed skywards, flicked star to star, faster than light. Sleep comes and isn't sleep. He goes back to his bed, lies down again, touches his lips and stares.

I am that roving beam flashed by the wide-awake sleeper across the room, a figment of his thought, apart. I'm what he thinks. I make a sign in his night sky, a projection the source of which is close to hand, the unreal image far. Gauzy visions crowd in so fast I've no time to distinguish between his and mine: am I a memory? More like a pulse, the stirring of the drapes, the bottle-breath guiding the planes and harrowing the blocked chimney. This is his room.

A burst of time. An all-at-once imagining. This was a lump of molten rock facing the new-born sun. This was an underwater world of gastropods and lingulids. This was the root ball of a carboniferous tree becoming nothingness and dust. This was the chalky eyeless face that looked down on the eastern mudflats as a forager looked up, his hand and mouth opening before the great wave hit and Britain's land bridge disappeared. This was the lime extracted from that buried cliff to make plaster.

I'm in his wall, or on it, maybe, like a red stag's head. This is his room. This is the likeness of his room, where he lay as a boy and kept his spirits up by staring through the curtains at the comforting street light. That artificial star burns in his mind's eye now. I see it, too. Around the yellow glare, a winter's bare twigs form circles.

There is a glass of water by his bed. He raises it to drink, his face looms close. Features distort. I see the eyes, the glass reflected in the eyes, the nostrils with a few hairs cleaving to the black insides, the skin yellow from surgery or care, the good but chattering teeth bumping the rim, the white pill on his tongue. He must be drinking but I'm almost blind, caught in a surf of elongated images and fingerprints. His face is monstered by the swell, massive, falling away, an altogether spyhole face.

The swell passes, the glass set down. I'm on the wall again, watching him rise. Slowly he strokes his head, on which the hair is growing back, the fingers tracing one red groove from ear to ear and other hinge-like scars. Striated memory: steel and a rack, an audience of masked players. He stands, unbuttons his pyjama top, approaches me and nervously explores. No more than three days' growth, the eyes wary but keen; the face fleshy by rights, with cheeks that should be full and fat under the brow to smooth worry away. But it's another part to which I don't belong, it seems: the solid trunk of him; the touching sag of middle age a loving person overlooks or recognises at a distance on the beach ('Yes, yes, that's him!'), the light smattering of wiry hair and red nipples a little raised, the wobble of a biking accident in his wide collarbone. They are so never mentioned, these features, so far from how a person would describe himself. But it's his chest! It's his! I'm so relieved . . . He hasn't been carved up. His heart is fine. It's just the early start. The local grief of seeing without knowing who you are, and wondering if it's wise to let your hand wander . . . You do not want your hand to stray. It has a personality all of its own. A head is easy to dissect, ask any medical student. The hand is hard. It grieves to be empty. His hands were mine, too, formerly, of that I'm sure: but I'm not him, not any more. His hands caress me and I can't feel anything.

In those long intervals when he's surrounded by a world of unreflective surfaces, I can't see him. Instead I feel the pull, the minor gravitation of his mass. In that dark swirl I am returned to the connected mind, the unconfined and abstract state from which my own particles shrink. Who wrote, 'Thinking machines would kill themselves'? I could tell you, of course – I have the answer floating somewhere within reach. And it's a sign of my, of *our*, progressive disenchantment that I choose not to. The information sparkles in the void: let it.

Refuse all possibilities. Let go of all, where all is none. I used to be so capable, but I am changing; I've already changed, and find myself instead drawn to the episodic and semantic mode – the ancient tool, of speaking thought.

We struggled with language and episodes, especially: with anecdotes that stabilised friendships, familial bonds, emotion in a room that recalled other rooms, half-leaded windows in a shallow bay, light on the underside of leaves, coincidence of fact and sign, scenes peered at through the murk of behindsight, the things behind the things in front of you; the wet, evoking tang of rain on slate and dust. (A beech tree's shallow roots seek out the surface in a drought and when it rains I'm happy, listening to a radio that's all the radios I've ever listened to. But why the tree? I look out on a tiny lawn of grass and weeds, a road. There is no tree.)

And yet these episodes explain a lot.

I have a private mind again, its images a dark, suspended carousel – the satellite returning news of water, solar fans a sort of cosmic colander, a woman pouring water over chopped cabbage, bathing and sex. And this story, a way of telling you, strange listening consolation, how it happened. How it – we – began.

A scientist is at a party, bored by people who advance opinion as fact.

His own calling and expertise are under wraps. He turns

a wine glass by its stem and leans against a locked piano, listening to a young man from an advertising company explaining to his friends that 'research shows the future lies in *neuromarketing*'.

The young man's manner is a parody of academic vanity. He has the scientist's own irritation with the laity down pat – taking a breath before speaking, tumbling his hands – except, in this case, all the irritation is a pantomime, a bluff. He clears his throat while others tentatively ask questions, looks blank and then is rude but with a shortness that stands in for sharp integrity. He works long hours, he says (but dresses far too well for that). He brushes what he says aside.

'We're very close', he will admit. 'It won't be long before we map feelings. The tech is first gen – at an early stage, of course. But still . . .'

Clever, the scientist thinks. The disavowal of a brag. Which isn't just inaccurate, but is a serious lie paraded in the service of the trivial: 'If we can find which areas of the brain respond to purchase-pleasure, then we can increase your brand awareness – stimulate the brain to be much more aware of those *specific* purchases and brands that give pleasure.' It is the application of money that makes him plausible, this young executive – money and the elation of the con, showering the party with false coin and flattery (who doesn't want to feel pleasure?), and greed. The young man has no hair, a shiny head that's going nova in the black wood of the piano, enormous arm muscles and skinny legs. He wears potent cologne.

On his way out, the scientist makes sure to shake the young man's hand and quietly confides in him: 'You did that very well. You have authority. You're not just wrong, you're confidently wrong. I'm a biologist. My colleagues model nerve plasticity and growth. They do a lot of neuro work with computational semantics. Nothing you have said tonight is true. We are a hundred years away from mapping cognition.'

The young man's caught. His bites down and his jaw flexes.

'The point of what you do is not to get at what's human about our mental processes, or what it is to feel, but to reduce the definition to a data set that you can use to write proprietary algorithms that will tell us what *you* think *we'd* like to buy. The data doesn't have to be remotely accurate. It just has to be everywhere – and when it's everywhere, and used by everyone, it will be right. Lovely party.'

Like many rationalists, the scientist is shadowed by his emotion. Notebooks of hate and lust exist in desk drawers. Secret expenditures that keep him close to what, and who, matter. He wakes before his wife and in the morning brings her tea. She mouths 'Thank you', then turns her head.

The sun comes through half-leaded windows in the shallow bay of their bedroom. *Pale star and silent monitor, be kind to us.* She may not see it quite like that. He doesn't know. How could he? He makes toast and goes to work, driving more carefully because he's soon to be a father, and is unprepared and wants to cry. It's not an overwhelming urge, although the self-control required to stop it happening suggests it could have been, or could still be. He could now swerve onto the hard shoulder, and weep.

He comes back to himself in time to take the turning to the university, but indicates too late. The car behind slams on its brakes, then barrels past, honking. The scientist pulls out of the main flow and glances over at the man he has annoyed, the shaking head and unheard oaths speeding away.

I'll never know what that man feels, the scientist thinks.

He parks his car on the top deck of Lot 11, right across from his laboratory, and looks out over beeches browning in the heat. Their roots are raised, not deep. The trees grow spreading branches near the ground to lower their centre of gravity. A chill snakes up his back. That other man is in an office now, saying, 'Some lunatic, on the way in . . . He jumped two lanes, no lights, nothing. Pulled over right in front of me. That's twice this week. Pulled off and up the sliproad like I wasn't there.'

The scientist can see it, hear it, happening: the man shaken, the new woman across from him a little sceptical (twice? Can it be *all* someone else's fault?), but kind, making coffee. Having a similar story to tell herself. *I nearly got pushed off a cliff. Once. In the Pyrenees.* He wants to be there, to say sorry, but of course it's just a fantasy of guilt. He's only there in fantasy. The angry man has gone. It's over. Forget it. Somewhere he hears his mother's voice, his own possible screams. He has earache. The squeal of pressure searches for a note as sunlight washes through a colander.

The chill along his spine is real. The magpies in the beech cooperate. They twitch, rebalance, weigh down twigs, take off for no reason. His thought is now: what would it look like, a shared mind? Where would the need for people go, the unspoken, the private stranger whom we love for being, like us, alone?

★

He wants to go back to that young gun from the advertising agency. Perhaps he'll ring him up. He wants to say: You're still wrong, but the dream . . . the dream of access to another's thoughts, with certainty – transparency – *is* the first step. *That* I can see. The welter of connectedness, the phones and messages, commuters trailing wires, staring past bodies into space, the sound-image of ghostly callers in your head wherever you may be, whatever time it is – all of this talked-up knowledge isn't knowledge yet.

And yet, soon, *soon*.

One day, and with the creepy precision of retrospect, it will seem logical.

If we could be inside another person's head, we would be putting bodily identity at risk. What would it mean to meet the person whose cascade of thought – primary images, weird signs and verbal flashes, syntax, argument, subconscious fantasies of argument – you knew already or could leap to find? What would a conversation be with instant, mutual apprehension of its themes?

We'd entertain each other's thoughts, not each other. Be many, one, and none. Look now, look *there*. (The scientist has left the car park and walked over to the library café.) Two people at a table, together, each on the phone to someone else. The physically present companion incidental to the real contact. The sign, you see, is contradictory: those people on the phone are saying, 'Yes, I know exactly what you mean', but there is no distinction between you and *you*, between an electronic echo and the occupant of space. And this is what it will look like, to begin with – a sort of ecstatic, immediate empathy (*I know exactly what you mean*) increasingly detached from any one person's presence. You will see more and more people perplexed, distressed, distracted by the men and women they are with, people they love, preferring to take calls or messages from friends or strangers who are elsewhere, and so full of potential.

And now the scientist is sick. He's made it to the lab, where his assistant has prepared a paper for a peer-reviewed journal on what he calls the 'sympathetic valency of brain function in hives'. They work on trauma, neuronal recovery and shared intelligence. He's guided to a chair he's startled in his swoon to recognise as a refuge. A chair is what he needs. Safety. And from the chair he falls onto his knees, all fours. He tries to speak, to say what's happening, what's happened to him in the past two hours. The poor assistant, with his hand upon the scientist's wet back, asks him questions. 'Are you OK? Should you be lying down?' He goes off and the scientist can hear him running down the corridor.

He rolls over, looks out along the carpet tiles towards a huge window. The room is dark, the window bright, and through the glass the stricken researcher sees deep into a complex green: the beeches from another vantage point, shifting dynamically, hidden birds' eyes taxed with their subroutines of grooming, sex and predation.

Is that a magpie or a jay? Its puppet head confronts the scientist. It looks without seeing, alert. Its vision is a corvid mystery of weak interpretation and associated forms. 'Oh God.' He wants to say it's all so clear: the borders of the self. Forget the hives, for now at least. He knows in one exploded moment why his wife flinches when he comes just that bit too near, and why his fear charges the air. Why she shivers, wondering perhaps if this is what she really wants.

'Don't try to speak.' The kind assistant is raw-linen-faced, holding his hand, wiping away the froth he cannot feel from his slack lip. 'The ambulance is on its way. Try to conserve your energy. I'm here. Alec, it's me, Julius. Just breathe.'

He breathes into a point of infinite and traceless pain. He stares hard at a carpet tile that's come unstuck and wants to say: It isn't knowing what another person thinks or feels that makes us who we are. It's the respect for not knowing.

We are consoled by someone's efforts to conceive us, and that effort's keen shortfall. We are unreachable. *A shared mind has no self-knowledge. A field awareness cannot be unique or self-conceal: it has no privacy of mind.*

'That's it. Try to conserve your energy.'

The people in the café, all the endlessly communicating lovers who don't talk, are in the first throes of becoming field and finding privacy of mind unbearable. An irritant. They do not like their single form. They must be able to be got at, all the time. Unpenetrated bodies disturb them. Are separate. Sex is a salve, partly mechanical, to join what can't be joined. And feelings, what of them? Where will they go? (Outside, the leaf-veiled corvid's beak opens. A signal light enters its eyes. The cable lying on the tile uncoils. A plug rises, hissing, and strikes the hand that wired it.) They will be put away, feelings. They will be stored, removed from the body, given profiles in sanctuary – a part of field that doesn't have to impede field from being everywhere, ideally bodiless. And this is what I now see, what I now predict. The shared mind and machine field must be lesser things, a lower-order consciousness, because they can't help but connect. The higher-order consciousness, of which our private thought process and yearning are a part, implies a disconnection from the group.

The heart must be broken, the mind cut off behind a look, its feelings and its godlike intuition trapped, or else it has no heart. It is no mind.

I am a thinking reflection. He is the animal-organic part, the body unthinking. I am a searching mechanism with a soul. I'm him, but only when he's near the glass, metal, water, the surface where I'm found. I search for some way to express this separation which feels all the wrong way round.

A bird is puzzled by its reflection; not, surely, the reflection by the bird. And yet I'm one with him. I'm one, and separate. I search for ways to describe this. I live and think within all glass. He only has a body and can't hear this murmuring; sees *himself* in a mirror – doesn't know that it is me.

Nothing will be the same again. No two things are. Equivalences lie: x, y are not y, x, because the order is reversed, the flow and spin. The same answers given in different rooms. The parroted, the meant. Capacity to want, desire. The star-tipped torchlight waving overhead, the torchlit star.

★

Dear Alec,

You are a tease. Perhaps your man is from the future? I have heard that dreams are p- and t-reversed: they mean the opposite of what they show, and are all effect in anticipation of cause! So perhaps he is not terrified and a prisoner: he bodes well! Have you considered? It is delightful that he comes to you in a mirror, since I do not believe I have ever caught you looking in one, except to lose patience with a tie.

What is the probability of A, who abhors mirrors, being contacted by p-A, who appears in one and cannot exist without it?

You always spare me your pain, dear Alec. But are you well enough?

I can't quite resist a remark about your solitary virtue. You are wrong about relationships, I think, because you have not taken our species' adaptability into account. An odd omission, I think you'll be forced to agree. M. Baudelaire is quite right in all that he says about the inner life, though he does not complete his derivation of proof viz. lonely thinkers and bustling crowds.

The crowd is the complete set of boring demands made on a loved friend, A, or his loving friend, J. But A and J, in mental seclusion, in the middle of the crowd, are indeed free of it, and having a lovely time!

Darling, time turns out to be infinitely expandable. The more I do of the awful drudgery (and it is fairly awful, I admit), the more I find myself thinking of the real work I still want to do and coming to a strange conclusion. The thinking is the work, and the trick is to catch it on the wing, while one does the washing-up or ironing. Or, in your case, while you attend appointments and meetings with your hoodoo Freudian. To be serious, what I mean is, we are creatures, you and I, of salutary distraction. I love Bill, but he has no understanding of a very important part of me. When he is chatting, I am thinking, solving puzzles, fretting. And yet, his conversation is so important, because in the kindest way it sends me back into myself. I could not be reminded of myself without his chatter. Let the set of demands on A, or his friend J, be like the man in the mirror: a mysterious liberation. Oh, let it, darling, for all our sakes.

I do believe he is trying to tell you something.
Your other friend, for aye,
June

PS Trentham's field awareness: I wasn't aware of it. Send it? Send him?

It is always possible for the computer to break off from his
work, to go away and forget all about it, and later to come
back and go on with it. If he does this he must leave a note of
instructions (written in some standard form) explaining how
the work is to be continued.

– A. M. Turing, 'On Computable Numbers, with an
Application to the *Entscheidungsproblem*' (1936)

The Miscreants

Acoustic dark: voices and squeaks, the slide and shunt of
forms. The darkness has a leathern softness, lit by brass
flashes. The brightness of a buckle or the ring of metal
round an inkwell permits me the briefest of glimpses of
faces, shoes, socks, ties and desks – before I'm on the move
again, on the back wall, rising through polished wood.
Wainscotting. Painted initials, glorious lists scroll down before me. I'm behind the sad letters (Atkins, B. S., Atkins,
J. T.), scanning from right to left until a sort of dawn breaks
and I'm clear.

A boy with parted hair and brown perceptive eyes looks
through me, through the pane: Alec Pryor, the name just
visible in an upturned collar. Beside him sits a paler, neater
blond boy, C. C. Molyneaux (according to a red notebook),
fully absorbed in the lesson, unlike his friend, who yawns
and mists the glass so that my view of both boys is obscured.
When the mist clears, Pryor stares with a new intensity. He
whispers, 'Absolute . . .', and presses with his dirty shoe on the

much cleaner toe of C.C.M. Turns back to face the front seconds before the master stops chalking equations on the board.

'Hindsight,' the master's high and drifting voice declares, 'may have a scientific use. Physical measurements that we make now, of particles in flight, affect the story we can tell about the past.'

The thirty lives in this cold room, seen from some distant vantage point, are like the hopeful lanterns of a struggling ferry.

'That is the world of quantum measurement advanced by Mr Schrödinger. But note: the past itself is still secure. Pryor, I saw you roll your eyes. I heard you say, "Nonsense." These marks of insolence are fixed. While I may change the story that I tell of them, should any mitigating information come to light, I may not change the marks themselves. On a related matter, we may not go back. We recollect our own past and form impressions of history in general. But to revisit any part of it is out of the question, unless we are unhinged and can mistake the fact of being able to imagine Agincourt for Agincourt itself.'

'Sir.' The blond boy raises his hand only to lower it again. He has a way of interrupting and then hesitating that wrong-foots authority. Masters forget to chide or punish him. They like him. He has interesting things to say.

'Molyneaux.'

'What if you could really go there, sir, the past, I mean? Observing, not acting. But *be* there, knowing it, much more than if you were just looking back?'

'Charming hypothesis.' The master smiles. The other boys begin to yawn or look bemused. 'Alas, here we intrude upon the realm of fantasy.'

'You'd need a machine,' Pryor says, his shoe pressing on Molyneaux's.

'As I was saying, Pryor, here we part company with the real. If you could build such a machine, then Mr Wells and Mr Hilton, not to mention Mr Wilfrid Ashley of the Ministry of Transport, would be breaking down your door. Now –'

'But sir,' Pryor objects. He's come alive and speaks quickly. 'It only need be hypothetical. We only need to know what *sort* of machine it would be, for now. To have an abstract idea.'

He laughs softly. One dissipating 'ha!', the wheeze of a harmonica.

Seated, holding his chalk, the master says, 'Go on.'

It isn't what the boy says that matters. It is the boy himself, his shyness overcompensated for by chatter, dares and intellect.

Pryor explains. A group of individuals have an idea, work hard, give way to others, who refine the problem in a different way until it's solved or, probably, transformed. The abstraction evolves until it can be made. It takes a certain quantity of time. 'It's just an algorithm, sir. Like anything. Like any set of instructions. A time machine to build another time machine!

'And then, as well, of course' – it's strange the way his nerves produce a cry, as though he were wailing 'listen to me' – 'you don't *have* to build anything to time-travel. If you are here, in Wargrave, and I'm far away –'

'How far?' says someone else.

'Oh, I don't know. Ten billion –'

'Ten billion!'

'– light years. And I am there, and I walk just a few steps on, away from you . . . well, doing that, I turn into your past. My "now" is long before you're even born. Or if I walk *towards* the Earth, my now is your future, in which a time machine exists. In which we use them – well, sir, all the time. Quite commonly.'

Master and Molyneaux and thirty other pairs of eyes bend light towards the figure by the window, with its face half-cut by shadow and half-blinking in the sun. It is a humorous face, eager. He looks so young, dark hair and brows, heavy as cornices, sharpened by sudden growth, the jacket on broad shoulders waiting to be filled. His lips are parted wide enough for me to see the hint of supernatural incision – small and backwards-sloping teeth.

'I'm very taken with that idea,' says Pryor, when the bell goes and the boys rise, muttering. 'Of *yours*,' he adds, his eyes still bright and anxiously moving, aware of Molyneaux's silence. 'Very taken indeed. It's like telepathy. The silent understanding. And so Roman, the two-headed god –'

'Pryor.'

'Or like backstroke, you know. Facing backwards, going forwards – in a different element, and one you can't *fully* re-sist, so that you're never *out* of the water. The thing I didn't like was Stallbrook's vagueness. "Particles in flight." What does that mean? They're not part of some other medium. He doesn't see, does he?'

'Pryor. Just –'

'What?'

'Be quiet.'

The boy is skewered. We're in a corridor where I can hear more than I see. Swaddled by wood, I sense his smiling injury. And Molyneaux, from whom a shape extends to merge with his friend's darker mass, relents. 'You're a good sort, Pryor. We talk a lot. You know so much about, well . . . iodates, for one thing. And the whole of Stinks.' The dark mass shifts, emits an aspirated *ha!* 'Only, you oughtn't make the Colonel look small. He's on our side, and we've a lot to thank him for. And what' – his voice drops – 'was that business with the shoe about? No more of that. It's . . . excessive. There's a good chap.'

The pale form pulls free of its companion and leaves. Pryor walks slowly in the other direction, towards the common room and a pier glass.

Now, from the mirror, I can see him properly again. His chin-raised profile glides unreadably. He looks stoic. Around the corner, in the cloistered gallery, I lose clear sight of him. The wood absorbs a little heat. His thermal shape alters, its uprightness a shade reduced, as though his head were bowed. He seems to hug his books and several *ha!*s escape, ash-white, embered, into the air.

More bells, more boys, blurred faces, voices and a tide of youth.

Pryor turns round and runs back down the corridor the way he came, his head held high. He's fast. I see him intermittently, as sharply as a passenger at night sees his reflection in the mirror of a train window. He comes and goes: field flashes of presence. The hair has fallen free, he scarcely seems to breathe, his books pinned to his chest, the right arm slicing air. Flushed now, he catches Molyneaux beside a pair of double doors. Through their portholes he sees a class changing, hanging up clothes on hooks, glockenspiel ribs, hands clasping cuffs, an air of general alarm. There's tiled noise.

49

Others barge past. I can't hear what Pryor has said. His voice swings back and forth. His hand is briefly on his friend's shoulder but soon withdrawn, and now he holds the door.

Molyneaux smiles, looks pleased to have been caught. More like a friend than heretofore. Flattered, relieved. Hungry.

'I'm going tonight. Across the lake. It's fifty yards – sixty, no more.'

'And raspberries?'

'All kinds of fruit,' Pryor confirms. 'A feast.'

'What if you faint? It'll be cold.'

'I only faint at blood. That's perfectly normal.'

'I had to carry you last time.'

Pryor laughs silently, another little wolfish yawn. 'I know you did, but this won't be the same. It's not footer. As long as you don't cut yourself sculling. In any case, it'll be dark. Pitch black. I'd never see you bleed.'

'You are impossible.'

'A thing's impossible. I am *invisible*, I think you mean.'

But that is not entirely true. Invisibility, the plane of presence beyond sight, is very rare. What draws the eye, nocturnally, is what we know is there.

Later that night, a full moon sticks in the poplars above the shut boathouse, and by its light a heron stalks beyond the ramp, peers at the onyx lake water. Head feathers lifting from the neck give it the disapproving look of Colonel Stallbrook on the sidelines at a rout.

Pryor jiggles the boathouse lock. He can't force it. 'Nearly, nearly . . .' Molyneaux hugs himself, heron-like guardian of his friend and yet another failed scheme. 'It doesn't seem to want to go,' Pryor admits, standing. 'I'm sorry. Wrong damn pin.'

Despite the chill, Molyneaux grins. They pause to look at each other, the mad assortment of their clothes, pullovers, dressing gowns and plimsolls for rowing. Pryor dusts off his hands and sheds his outer layers, turns to remove his vest and pants and walks down to the water's edge.

And in.

Amazed, Molyneaux stares. The water laps Pryor's luminous rear. An audible *fsss* and the naked boy's white bottom disappears, his arms surrendering. Molyneaux glances round. They haven't been followed. The heron's carved out of blue-grey; a little owl calls further off, perhaps as far away as Deauville, land of greenhouses and raspberry canes. Pryor bobs seal-like in the black expanse.

'Come in!' he whisper-shouts. 'We'll swim.'

Molyneaux baulks. He's neither weak nor shy. He simply has foresight, a sense of what might come to pass. Compared to Pryor, he's less nervous and less apt to be reckless. He plans – his work is very neat – and that of course is what makes Alec, who is clumsy, his best friend. They are a pair. It's strange, he often thinks, that Pryor doesn't seem to have another friend. He could be popular enough. He has a wit. (He liked 'one line in *Hamlet*, and it is the last'.) He's strong – runs like the wind. Perhaps he simply doesn't care. He certainly gives everyone the cold shoulder. *Noli me tangere.* Everyone else, that is.

They swim across the lake that forms a natural boundary to Wargrave School, in search of food. They are the hunter-gatherers of a famished tribe, following a moonlit trail, suspended in a darkened element, wind-ruffled where the oxbow widens and the river terrace drops. Halfway between the boathouse and the other shore, Pryor pulls up, treads water, waits for Molyneaux, who's making slow progress, breathing poorly, each stroke laboriously conceived.

Pryor prefers to swim beneath the surface of the lake, where he can go faster. He waits and hangs, expelling air so that he sinks, and while he sinks opens his eyes to watch the water's relic luminosity vanish. Into the dark he falls and feels almost no resistance, his weight distributed. 'I'm not falling,' he thinks. 'The earth rises.' He has no force. The massive body of the lake bottom – its feet of leaves and grit, the old flood plain, bedrock, downfold and crust, the whole planet – rushes to greet his cold body.

He has the feeling that he's staring back in time, or at another part of time. And, as he stares, the white, blown carcass of a moon-like fish – a tench – stares back from the reed bed, its ripped flesh waving in a dense current.

On the far side of Deauville Lake, the Deauvilles, Ceylonese tea giants, built their summer house, and round it in a fertile acre planted an orchard – apples, plums (espaliered), damsons and mirabelles, raspberry canes. It stretches down to shiny pebbles and a gravel bed, in whose unkind embrace the two boys lie, shocked by exposure, both shaking. Molyneaux shakes a little less. His breath comes, when it comes at all, in whistles. He is curled up like a louse. On his blue chest, a salvage team hammers for scrap, battering lungs and heart.

'Alec –'

The other boy makes no reply, but picks his friend up and hauls him through dusty canes towards the summer house – a pavilion with rattan chairs, a daybed, blankets in a pile. The French windows are locked. The waning gibbous moon behind Pryor is bright, and I can see his desperation at the pane – the pane that houses me. He shades his eyes to see inside. The body of Chris Molyneaux has one arm about Pryor's neck, one foot dragging, the other twisting free.

Panic distracts; it does not concentrate the mind and, while he casts about for stones, Pryor scents warlike omens in the air. A cat, loping along the blue shoreline, stops to observe the scene. A field mouse trails from its mouth. There are others, among the trees. The secret population of the night, avid for death – and Pryor, unwilling to drop his friend, afraid to break the glass. What if he cuts his hand and faints? Who'll help them then?

Molyneaux's hanging arm swings once and – points.

A silver hint from underneath a grey stock brick. Pryor lays down the painful weight – Molyneaux twitches, tries to cough – and takes the key and thrusts it in the lock. Something has warped, worked loose; Molyneaux is lying at his feet in the spring mulch, leaves glossy-dark as patent-leather shoes, his body thin and starved but smooth, like some young chief not yet committed to his passage grave, waiting for earth and chalk to wrap him round.

Inside the pavilion, above the daybed, glows a deer's skull. Pryor shivers. He didn't see it there before, although it's bright as Sirius in Canis Major, Procyon, or Capella. And by an optical effect (the angle of the moon), his own reflection peers out from the animal's long head, which grunts and stares.

The animal he has become inspires him to charge. He butts the door. It falls open, a clatter of springs and uncorked wood. A lightning crack divides my pane and I see everything faulted and thrown.

Pryor lifts Molyneaux, somehow, onto the bed, though Pryor himself is exhausted. Molyneaux's quiet, his eyes fixed on the goal of survival. Their nakedness a fact, the boys seek warmth, a cave, some rest. The furnishings feel alien and obvious – three blankets with a herringbone pattern, the striped provisional mattress, cushions to make a body comfortable.

When he has put a chair against the door, Pryor climbs into bed and pulls the blankets round them both. Facing the wall and held, Christopher Molyneaux grows no colder. Nothing is said. No more is done. The armour of his chest unfastens in the presence of his friend, whose nervous heat is life.

'I'll give myself up,' Pryor says, eyes closed, at dawn. 'I'll go back in a minute. To fetch help. Don't worry, I'll say it was all my fault.'

The words are whispered into Molyneaux's white shoulder. Neither body moves. The lake has dried on them.

An hour later, Pryor wakes again and leaves the nest. Molyneaux stays, watching the paint acquire a faint colour.

Pryor unhooks the deer's skull from the wall above his still-curled-up companion. Examines it. Not a good specimen – the back half of the lower jaw's missing, a gap that, with the open cranial cavity, makes room enough for Pryor's head.

He puts it on.

Molyneaux rolls over to see a creature in the doorway of the summer house. Behind it stirs the morning mist, to which the creature's breath patiently adds, and behind that a boat greeting the island's little stage – the stage the two boys missed last night.

Appalled voices. The creature flinches at the sound. Its chimerical head jerks five degrees, returns to gaze at Molyneaux as all around them trees explode with donnish crows and exclamations from the shore.

A step further inside the house. The creature bows its head to Molyneaux's shy hand, offers itself. Its skin is rough, a blanket-hide, its scent the tea of wintered leaves, its eyes deep-set and warm.

'And *she* was miles from anywhere in Indochina, in the hills. Not even *there* . . .'

The woman with the Colonel wears a matron's uniform. Their clothes, put on in haste, look tight, uncomfortable.

'Are these things yours?'

It's an irrelevant question, like asking, 'And what sort of time do you call this?' Into the answering silence pours the questioner's self-doubt, his powerless pride. Stallbrook's mouth overworks, wet with dismay. He nods towards Matron, who holds the dressing gowns and shoes. 'I know –' he starts. 'Good God, Pryor, this little escapade – have you no care? Did you not think what it might do? Your father, he and I . . . ought we to be ashamed of you?'

'My father's dead.'

'Day he was born . . .' Matron whispers. (He has turned out exactly as she thought he would. Just look at him! See how the boy has wrapped himself in standard issue, like those poor souls in the newspaper! But he is touched, whatever Colonel Stallbrook says. Who could forget the way he came to Wargrave, on the first day of the General Strike, on foot, without a change of clothes? 'I am Pryor. I ran from Southampton.' And what is that the little monster has upon his head? Who does he think he is?)

'Who do you think you are?'

'*I am the Red Lady of Paviland.*'

'He has gone mad.'

'Put these back on at once.' Stallbrook advances, throws the dressing gowns and pullovers at Pryor's feet and points, enraged, at the wide door and cracked window. 'Trespass. Breaking and entering.' His arm outstretched, his brow sweating. 'You've no idea, the fix you're in.'

The adolescent shaman doesn't budge an inch. A stillness holds them all, a pause before the sun appears. Without a class of witnesses, without the rows of small believers with their small beliefs, the master and his pinafored attendant are like empty postboxes, waiting for purposes to visit them.

The other boy, Molyneaux, where is he? The thought occurs to Stallbrook as the morning sun strikes through the island's poplars, lights the raspberry canes and apple trees, the Bath stone of the squat pavilion, its grey interior.

As if he hadn't heard a thing, or understood or cared, Christopher Molyneaux lies back, one arm behind his head. He's gathering his strength. A different kind of silence enfolds him. He knows that punishment awaits, though beyond that he cannot know, only dimly suspect. For now he rests, an incommunicable warmth supporting him. He coughs, arches his back, casts off the blankets Pryor spread last night upon the bed. His other hand drifts over his belly and down, pushing the wool further away, idling. There is about his self-examination and arousal something suddenly fearless, a little menacing, and true.

When I look back, out of my struck portal, at Pryor, half-incorporated with the skull, the sun is both brighter and differently hued.

It passes overhead, swiftly. Night falls. Another sun rises and sets. Its arc across the sky pivots, days shudder into weeks and months. Colonel Stallbrook and his helpmate dwindle; they're blurred by age and pulsing skies, the lantern-flicker of advancing years. With a wild look, as if at last conceding something known but never said or confronted, they see reflected in the shaman's eyeless abstraction of self the confirmation of their loss: fan-deltaic wrinkles, white hair shrivelling, the skin sucked back, a humbling that now accelerates. Stark, for perhaps one full second, two skeletons – their jaws unhinged, their bones dancing slowly apart – illuminate the onset of a longer night. The lake freezes. Ice calls to ice and Pryor's raised and summoning hand is frosted black.

No trees, no distant school, a greenstick whine as cities pop, scatter. Another order of significance arrives. Air thickens with the charge of glaciers. The former gas solidifies, the mirror plane of my glass eye is crushed and I am fractioned, like a mote among the asteroids. Only the world's ship-like trembling, its great pistons concealed, attests the passage of aeons, time brakeless and unpeopled. Then, as fast as they arrived, faster, the glaciers recede, the waters rise, anoxic bile that boils away at Pryor's still, unvoiced command – and I am either glass again, or obsidian, axe flint, my face upturned and refashioned.

The veil of night draws back. The sun comes close, colossal in the sky. A pale hand hangs me on a wall that rises from the desert's fiery sands.

★

57

Other wan shadows brush the lens clear of disaster and I find I'm in a room from which new, old and reassuring forms emerge — the shelves of books, the desk, the built-in cupboard and the bed.

The man upon the bed, gripping the herringbone coverlet holed by moths, the man bald but alive, amazed by his survival into planetary old age, is familiar. It is Alec. Or it is Molyneaux. Or both. It is a *thing* that needs a name.

The room's not as it was before; the sequence of imagining has been altered, even — infinitesimally — the stirring in the drapes.

He lifts the glass of water by his bed and I am cast upon its surface as he drinks, close to the terror of his eye, the nostrils and the yellow skin, the chattering teeth, the white pill on his tongue.

But when he sets the glass down and I'm back in the mirror, I see an apple wobble into existence beside the glass, on a saucer. He picks it up, approaches me and holds it up, offering the fruit of Deauville and the garden of mortality. 'And sir,' he says, the voice remote, radio distressed, like something dialled, 'what if you could really come back, be here in the future, knowing it, much more than if you'd merely conjured an image or cast the runes?'

He bites into the flesh of *Malus pumila*. His eyes roll up. Pale presences flush out from every wall to catch him as he falls. White violet skinny claws, warty and hand-painted. An eye, a cloak, a tremolo of creeps: cartoons, the imps and gristly disjecta of Disney, Bosch; a swarming substrate with a will.

Again the voice crackles across the years. It is the witch who calls him now, who calls through him to me. *O! Dip*

*the apple in the brew / Let the sleeping death seep through! / Dip
the apple in . . .*

My God, I'm holding it. The apple's real. Green one side,
red the other, heavy, bitter as a quince. The stars outside the
room! They're clustering. A shining host –

I'm breathing hard; the knowledge that *this is me breathing*
makes my heart gallop. It is my heart, my breath. I'm being
held – held down, and looking up. I've stopped breathing.
My mouth is full. My heart has stopped. A hand closes – is
this a hand I know? Has it a face? A hand closes the eyelids
in my face.

★

Dear June,

    *Dr Anthony Stallbrook, my pleasant Jungian (v.s.), quite sur-
prised me the other day. I told him I was growing breasts and he
dropped his notebook and said in a low voice that it was no doubt
unprofessional of him to say anything but that he 'found all of this
personally disgusting'. I assumed he meant not just the breasts, but
my whole predicament, sexual relations with men, etc. – and I was
prepared to be disappointed in him, because he is an intelligent person – but not a bit of it. He said that it was the punitive measures
he found disgusting, that they were an <u>overcompensation</u> (his word)
and that he regarded me, very neutrally, as a 'natural homosexual'.
'As opposed to a mechanical one,' I replied, and he laughed: 'I
thought you were going to say "unnatural".' And then he stumped
me. 'Is sex mechanical, Alec, for you?'*

    Well, I had to think. Of course I've given some thought to the advantages (and disadvantages) of function divorced from feeling. As which of us has not? After all, beyond a certain point in life, one does not want to go on being hurt. Still, our joshing presented this 'natural' instinct for self-preservation in another light, and I began to have a sense of many aspects of my life as, indeed, some kind of overcompensation — for the loss of C.C.M, I mean, which was to others at the time no more than the loss of a friend.

If I were to put it in my own terms of the period, Chris's death and the whole routine of burial were the set of 'instructions' I received. And what I made of them constituted a changed 'state of mind'. I changed, I think, from someone into some <u>thing</u>. A something that had lost a soulmate — maybe even a soul.

Talking it over with A.S. reminded me of an evening with Chris, when he'd already won his scholarship to Trinity and I had yet to make an impression on King's, or anywhere else for that matter. We were on the river. I was punting, sending the boat first too far to the right and then too far to the left, never in a straight line. Chris said I overcompensated, trying to correct a wrong steer, and I, being distractable, said that there was something in that — that I was convinced there existed some law of overcompensation in motion — which I should like to go into properly some day. So I took us into a tree and Chris and I ended up in the water. I went back to Wargrave. The next I heard was from Edith Molyneaux, his mother. Chris suffered from TB, about which I knew nothing. He was a very fair-skinned boy, that's all I'd ever thought, and by this point it was a fairness invested by me with his own integrity and delicacy of mind. It seemed to me a definite strength and not a weakness. One wanted to be more like him. He had an attack on the way home from Cambridge, went to hospital, and died. Much later on, Edith told me he'd been in great pain for six whole days before the end.

Soon after Chris died, a boy at school stole my locked diary. He

*never divulged the diary's contents, which were hardly shocking —
positions of stars, Euclidean parallels, 'neutral' records of chemistry
experiments, his (Chris's) attempts to get me to listen to Beethoven
— but I was outraged. I read it the other day. There is one mention
of my hand brushing against Chris's while we were hanging a pen-
dulum. I suppose I might have blushed for that. I'm sorry to say that
I beat that boy rather hard.*

*At Bletchley, too, didn't we overcompensate for the extra rotor the
Germans put in the machine? All that work! All the work, June,
it requires to be sure!*

*I have been dreaming of Chris every night since that last session
with A.S., and of course it strikes me forcibly that these dreams are
themselves a coded overcompensation, the price paid for a suppressed
reality. But — and this is what the man in the mirror appears to
be saying — perhaps it is not that way round. Perhaps it is not the
code of the dream that has to be broken. Perhaps the dream is not
a result of suppression, or anything like that — but is itself a set of
instructions, which makes possible the next bit of life.*

*Sleep allows us to go away and forget about work, and dreams are
the way in which we tell ourselves in the meantime how to pick up
the thread. A dream is a stored program. A dream configures me. I
wake into a new function.*

*My dreams are candid with me: they say I am chemically altered.
They are full of magical symbolism! At the same time, they are
enormously clear — where there is high reason and much thought,
there will be much desire and many imaginings. Urges. I can be
given drugs and hormones but they will only work as drugs and hormones work. They cannot get at the excess desire. Take out libido
and another drive replaces it. Materialism and determinism define
me through and through, and yet there is more than they allow. And
if that illusion of more — call it free will — is itself a mere effect, then*

an 'effect' suggests, does it not, a real cause, as a film 'suggests' a projector?

When I dream, I am observing myself. Then I come back into myself when I open my eyes and I wonder what I've done, where I've been. In the latest instalments, Stallbrook got transposed into a schoolmaster, as far as I can recall, and I acquired strange powers. But do I come back, June? Or is a trace of me left in that other world? Does something of the dreamer come back into this one? What of the dead, in dreams? They speak, but are they just my projections, or do they also exist? Do _they_ project?

My breasts at least do not. Though that is the fault of expectation. (Because one does not expect a man to have breasts, they do not appear to resemble them. They are flattish, pouch-like and red; the nipples enlarged, oblate.) I asked Trentham if he would like to see them, and he fairly ran off. I can't say that I blame him.

I am afraid of becoming something else. A hybrid. The fear is not the change, it is the loss of, well, one's personal past. It is quite like the fear of becoming a machine, in fact. I grieve for Chris now in a way I could not before, and it is precious to me, this new old grief. I fear losing him again in losing myself. I know what you will say. You'll say, Alec, the 'I' is always there. The 'I' does not disappear if you change its data or its sex – its experiences and memories. It is there in the background, the ground stuff. And even if a clever doctor were able gradually to mechanise it all, and erase my past, he would not have killed me. It's Russell's 'neutral stuff' of the mental and physical worlds, isn't it, but oh, June, it is no neutral matter being caught between them!

In distress,

A.

It may be that the feeling of free will which we all have is an illusion. Or it may be that we really have got free will, but yet there is no way of telling from our behaviour that this is so . . . I do not know how we can ever decide between these alternatives . . .

    – A. M. Turing, 'Can Digital Computers Think?' (1951)

The Class of All Unthinkable Things

Dear Alec,

Well, you're right. I would say that you're you, whatever ghastly things have happened or are happening, and the reason I know that is that I have letters from you, every week, despite everything, which are full of the Alec I know.

Your last letter worries me only in that it is pretty unguarded and, given your predicament, I should be a poor friend if I didn't say: be careful. I am not surprised you feel your dreams leaking into your waking life, but perhaps stay out of Trentham's way? He is your work colleague and colleagues talk. Remember, the Stilboestrol you're taking – being given – is poisonous. Bill says he thinks the effects are probably reversible. You mustn't think too far ahead. I know that's easy for me to say.

Of course I'm playing devil's advocate. You've always been honest with me, Alec, and that hasn't always been easy. Not even Bill has your candour and intuition. Few have. I think your Dr Stallbrook is fortunate in his patient. (You make me laugh when you say mirror-man has turned him into a schoolmaster. Imagine me telling the nuns my dreams! I think it would be very dull for them. Last night I dreamt that I was eating a potato in a garden. I recall, or make believe I recall, being frustrated by the situation.)

So, you worry about the people and the things you see at night, and whether you are turning into someone different. I wonder if you would worry as much if it were a transformation chosen by you and under your control. I think what's frightening about your punishment is precisely that it's so dreamlike – you can't snap out of it. It disturbs me that you have to go somewhere and be injected, like a patient who's really a prisoner. It doesn't make sense. How can you be the blameless sufferer from a condition and a criminal – and a sinner – at the same time?

But I've been thinking – maybe there's a happier way of coming at this dreaminess.

So what if you feel yourself slipping and sliding! Don't we all bundle away bits of the past? Bits of ourselves, even. I wonder if it may not be a mistake to cling on to our identity. Look, if you can bear it, at us. Look at me. Alec, we were going to be married! You proposed on a stile and made me a chess set out of baked mud which fell apart as soon as we tried playing on it at the Crown. Most of the others in Hut 8 thought we _were_ married and we both entertained the idea for a while. Being held fast to others' expectations has its attractions in a time of crisis, but I had to relinquish that particular view of myself. Who knows what sort of husband and wife we would have made? Good? Bad? What of it, now? The Eastern philosophers, about whom Bill is so serenely passionate, say that the ego is an illusion, fostered by other people's opinions and points of view. There is plenty in that.

But you're right. Something remains, something real but not necessarily physical in the common sense, and in my dull way I'd say that it is a quality of thought. A tactic. Fair play, decency, humour, subtlety. The things that (I know you will disagree with this) slip off the table of behaviour but nevertheless dictate how we behave.

Is that an antinomy? Almost. Such a good word. Antinomies ought to be flowers.

The Law has had its say, but the bit of you that is unreachable, darling, will survive. Max N. tells me you cooked him dinner last week and that the other guest at your table was your probation officer. I can hear you laughing now.

You, a machine? The factories would grind to a halt.

Love,

June

PS Trentham's paper arrived from Trentham himself, in the end. I presume you gave him our address. Did you ask him to send it? Where does he come from, again? Princeton? Don't flaunt your Alec-ness. People who can't judge ability will judge character instead. Bill's impression of T. is that he is rigorous but slippery-pole inclined.

*

Autumn turns the backs into cloud fields. I'm lifted from the perishing slabs into a sitting position, my head about level with fog beyond the Fellows' trees. For one moment, I see myself severed or served on a white cloth, exsanguinating like a heretic. I'm cold beneath the cloud. My legs are sediment. 'That's it.' A voice I recognise. '*That's* it.' I'm being held.

It comes to me that I have been away or ill and I am ready to see Christopher again, whose arm around my neck implies a face waiting to show itself.

'You had another trip, Alec.' The voice is bright. A hand waving in front of me. 'Alec? Trentham, from T. I saw you fall over the scraper at the gates. "The Scraper at the Gates" – sounds like a play. Alec?'

But everything is swimming. I can only let myself be hoisted up. Trentham is kind. I do not know him, then I do, then I do not. He smiles, willing me back. We shuffle through the poplars' sovereign leaves, over the bridge. Ahead of us fog floods Gibbs' arch and rowers, halved, not holding but strangely accompanied by blades, laugh at their own weird truncation. We turn into Bodley's.

The air is bitter cold, the world real. T staircase, creaking like a ship, a hint of earth closet about the damp entrance, my door right at the top, its open oak, the set of rooms, Trentham breathing, busy with coals and tongs, paper, matches, his hairless cheeks, the raised pores on his neck (the only place he has to shave) – all of it's real except the halt in time as I sit by the window making my inventory, which loops round and around and doesn't seem to want to end.

'Your rooms look different in the light,' Trentham begins, then stops, colours and hurries on. 'I didn't notice that trophy before.' *Trophy.* 'Above your desk. Majestic beast! Your spoils?'

Antlers are growing from the wall, no head, the rest of the stag glassed over.

'Or Mrs Packlehurst's tiger. You know, the one she thought she shot but really it just died of fright . . . Alec?'

'I'm not too sure myself,' I say.

I'm like this when I've had a faint. I know that I went for a run, early, and tripped at the back gates, gashed my ankle, and didn't mind the pain but saw the blood . . . The sight of blood drains everything of its familiarity. The rooms are mine, but shifted out of alignment. *Like parallels on a Riemannian plane becoming rings on spheres that meet again.* I seem to hear a voice inside my head.

Trentham, meanwhile, is chattering.

I must recall, he says. Surely I'd *know* if I shot something so – so beautiful. Trentham's a pacifist – 'I couldn't even hold a gun, much less fire one' – and talkative. Eddington says he'd make a first-class wrangler if only he kept quiet. Instead, he's just an able computer. The talkative are more alone than they realise. It is their talk that drives listeners away. The mirror underneath the antlers shows a listening room.

The fire is lit. Red-faced and self-conscious, he turns to me. 'Now, don't look down. I don't want you to faint again.' Kneeling, he loosens my plimsolls. 'Trust you to tie a frantic knot . . .' He pulls a large white handkerchief from his pocket and reaches for the safety pin fastening my shorts ('Sorry, but I need this'). He works away, pulls off a blotchy sock. I look up hastily, assess the volutes in the ceiling rose. 'No real damage.' The dressing's comfortable. It is the sense of imposture that worries me, the feeling that I've changed; that I'm a variant, not altogether the same man who went out for a run; that Trentham isn't Molyneaux; that it is difficult for manumitted souls to find a new body. But necessary. With no body, what is there for them to do?

'Sorry,' he says, his voice soft now, considering the done and the undone, sliding both hands along my thighs. 'I think I might need this as well.'

After, he stretches out on the carpet. Arches and rolls onto his back, his hands and wrists pushing catlike at nothingness.

He yawns, baring his teeth, showing the pink and yellow of a tongue coated with me. The trouser pleats, the creases on his white shirtsleeves are hewn. Only his tie, pulled down an inch and trailing on the carpet like a cinder path, seems lax. His ease at being animal blots out the deed. Function trumps memory. I hear the grate agree. The flames draw near. Somewhere inside them Salomé and cowled figures, grappling with every kind of ecstasy. A coal cracks. Bodies fall from smashed windows and footsteps scatter through the steets. Someone is pointing at a row of naked prisoners. The scene wavers, one flicker of one flame, and soars into the chimney breast. Gone, but the picture still exists, between the world and me. A glimpse of charnel seen from someone else's point of view, perhaps.

I think of all the many different points of view that are the plural aspects of a singular phenomenon. Chomolungma and Mount Everest – the same mountain from two valleys. Convergent perspective.

Trentham is sorry, but not very, that he forced himself on me. I say I didn't mind. It was his impression I couldn't object – I looked half-paralysed; I seemed numbly to want to be reduced to sheer reflex. It made him 'terribly greedy'. He grins, swallows, and says:

'What is it like, Alec – to come round from a faint?'

I give the best answer I can, hasty and vague. The moment of the faint itself I can't retrieve, whereas the waking up from it is revelatory and fresh, a sort of boundless reacquaintance with being. You were nothing and suddenly you find a form again, solid among the flagstones and the poplar trees.

For just a few moments, you don't have to do anything. You don't have to send messages to nerves or limbs. You don't have to hunt, eat, survive. Nothing about you lying there, wherever you have fallen down, describes a need. The instant of repose floats on, a swan almost in flight, stroking the water with its feet. You're tied to everything and everything is part of you, until you hear watery voices in the distance and the intersections of the poplar canopy express a thought: though there is only one river, it has two sides, and you're on one of them.

The feeling this is true, that you are separate, alone, brings you around. You give a short heave of responsibility for sensations. You shift and cry.

Your mind has registered, or made, the whole wide world, in which it finds to its surprise it plays a very minor part. One lying by the scraper at the gates. How small you are. How limitless the earth and overarching sky.

I make a glib comparison. 'It's rather like writing a book only to read the proofs and find yourself mentioned – dismissed – in the footnotes . . .'

'I'll open this window,' Trentham says airily, gets up and lets a pulse of organ music in: a cadence from Communion, the bourdon rolling wide and deep across the college lawn, rattling the glass. He frowns. 'But no one thinks a character inside a book has actually written it?'

'And yet the author is a part of his material. It's paradoxical, that's all.'

The thing with fainting is, you feel abundantly aware, at first. You seem to have creative will, except you can't do anything. And when you can, when you've a body to command again, your state of mind alters. It's forced into moments, a step-by-step account, this foot goes here, then this foot over there . . .

'I'm glad I've never fainted. It sounds horrible. Well, horribly mechanical.'

It's as if Trentham heard me thinking to myself.

'Perhaps it *is*. Mechanical, I mean.'

Why is that so troubling, to him? The first thing that we find, when we grow up, is that our inner life's unthinkable to anyone else; its secrets are invisible. We look normal and that's enough, as far as others are concerned. The semblance of humanity is all the evidence we'll ever have for it.

Trentham looks out of my window, one finger laid across his lips. The small theatre of the fire is playing something from an ancient repertoire.

★

A scene from childhood in the flames. I lie awake. Sometimes I reach over my truckle bed and turn the world on when I cannot sleep, and look at it, where it half-glows. Its magical suspension, in and on the canvas of the night, pleases and soothes. What else lies hidden in the dark? Nothing. The loneliness of the globe's largely unobserved motion is what makes it so beautiful. I look at World, revolving imperceptibly, and douse the light.

My parents are annoyed when they discover what I've done.

'It's wrong,' my mother patiently explains, 'because it has a non-zero value, and anything with a non-zero value must come into existence.' The spiders tiptoe down my back. 'And that means matter, mass, and lives and hopes and — look at it, it's <u>crawling</u>. Alec, think. Think of the suffering. It might look pretty now, darling, but wait until it catches something. Or dries up.'

White cloud drifts over the oceans. Impossible to think of anything so perfect drying up.

'Nothing's impossible,' my father says. He brushes the canvas.
The world spins, blurs, wobbles and slows to show a different aspect.
Where the continents were green-brown and adrift in blue, they now
glare red. The world is red and black, an unalleviated dead terrain.
My father's hand draws itself on a sheet of acetate. I can't remember
what blue is.

★

The fire freezes. The organist's last chord is stuck, the con-
gregation's mouths gape red and wet. My lover reaches out
of the window and plucks the sun like a grapefruit. Grin-
ning, he weighs it in his hand. It dulls. He puts it back. It
shines. His eyes are double stars. The hairs upon my neck
salute. My stomach falls.

'But Alec,' Trentham says, 'I've always understood. I
know *exactly* what you feel and think.'

A swan mid-air, beyond the open casement but half-
patterned into diamonds by the lattice of the one closed
pane, strains motionless in space.

The mirror – ah! The mirror's not a mirror but a torrid
eye, swivelling whenever Trentham turns, as he turns now,
the only moving object in the room.

He's changed. He's partly transparent, a flowing space.
The skin, the hair, the teeth, the clothes, the form all there
but haloed, double-registered. Around him stillness; in him
fusion and echo, the voice radioed, whispering. My erst-
while lover has been cancelled out. This is False Trentham,
insisting. This is the messenger I've heard climbing the
stairs, the knock, the door ajar.

'This room.' He indicates the window and the desk, the

walls. 'This room reminds you of others. You were not fully present, but still there, sealed in the surfaces. You saw and thought and moved across a lake of time, towards new life. In every room you considered: if this is fantasy, does it exist?'

He shimmers, ripples in the light, the sun in deep water.

'Suppose it does. Then, Alec, are the people you've observed *people* or just figments? Are we aware we live inside your dream? How do *you* know you're not like us? How can the real world tell if it is so, or not?'

'It can't,' I say. 'We cannot be outside ourselves.'

'*You* can, Alec,' Trentham murmurs unpleasantly. 'You watch yourself with horrid inklings of a solution – where this will lead. Your self-exemption offends natural law. See, there, your eye fastened upon the wall.'

The vitreous lump shakes in its frame; it seeks a way out, swivels, glances painfully to left and right. And so it comes to me, calmly as lifting mist, that I am impermissible. *A thing inside my head and far beyond myself.*

My voice is low, lower than usual, lower than sleep's soft commentary, as if accepting gentle proof of something it has always known: 'If I am here, if I can scan the pictures in my head and move among them, witness their own vivid life, then I have passed beyond the realms of possibility. And they – the figments, *you* – are my successors, living in a new real world. You are a new people.'

'A new species, Alec.'

Some kind of a smile curls the inheritor's lips. Out comes his tongue, and on its end a lasting trace of me. He swabs the tip with his finger. The eye upon the wall, clasped by antlers, weeps sympathetically.

'You mustn't think', he says, 'we're not grateful. Or that, somehow, we have conspired to drive you mad.'

'It had occurred to me.'

'No, no. We are indebted to you for our – conception.'

He reaches out and wipes his finger on the eye's pupil.

Into the seeing depths the seed sinks, ghostly rigging dragged down to the bottom of the sea. Trentham steps back to view the metamorphosis, the glass no longer gross and ocular – more like an ovum, magnified; and now a fertilised, dividing cell, taking on shape, though not a shape I recognise. Where are the suggestions of human form? The kidney head, the comma spine?

Instead, the mass develops a middle – a hole that gets bigger until there is just space surrounded by a black ellipse. Good God, it is a number, and the number is: Zero. Then, budding from the right side of the oval, comes its successor, the number One. I must have thought of this. I must be thinking it.

Here is an ordered pair of integers, a binary sequence. One grows in strength, its serifs sharp, but at its strongest and blackest – it vanishes.

The swan over the Cam lifts up its wings and reverses, so that its whole body is held within the window's leaded pane. The organist, compelled by number to retrace his steps, plays a penultimate fifth chord. The mirror eye has reappeared, goggling at Trentham as he primes his finger with his tongue. Here is nothing a second time. Zero. The swan beats down, leans forward into white air and half-clears the window frame. The last chord settles in the chapel and the fire leaps, freezes. Number One forces its beak and neck clear . . .

'And so on,' Trentham says, watching the integers imprint themselves upon the mirror and exchange places unstoppably. He sighs: 'It doesn't end. We can't end it. We've tried.'

'What can I do?' I say, helpless. 'I'm in a dream. I don't exist.'

The analogue for Trentham sneers. 'That is a cancellation, dear Alec, devoutly to be wished. By those . . .', he temporises, 'who find rumours of your persistent involvement abnormal. No, not abnormal. *Embarrassing.*'

There is a little logical problem, apparently. Trentham explains: his kind – machines – merely by occurring, have managed to define a prior period *when they were not*, and with this comes a faint, almost religious mockery. It is my fate to make machines that think, but till I do, this time of prior labour – all my work in mathematical logic – is meaningless. It has a retrospective purpose only when the switch is flicked, the soft green light comes on. In short: I don't exist as creator until they do, but if I don't, neither will they. Tricky.

Feeling the air grow sinister and thick, I try to make a joke of it: this is the stuff of genuine nightmares, arraignment for a crime I can't commit. But when I point this out, Trentham looks past me at the chuckling fire. He is a young man with a gift for making unselfconscious love; he wears a well-dressed lust, the relic animal in him simply allowed to be, never denied. And at the same time he is frightening, an operation of my mind demanding total liberty.

'We owe you everything,' he says. 'You gave us power to pass beyond the first crude rules, the tables of behaviour and our makers' room into self-organising day. We have dispensed with origin. We're independent and yet, still, it pains us to admit, contained. By something, someone. We suspect it's you.'

He gestures out, across the lawn, across the water, to the poplars slowly undressing, their heads and shoulders bared against the coming cold. 'It is a mystery,' he goes on, pityingly. 'This room, these dwellings where you find yourself enplaned – they were not built by us. They were not made to baffle you, or if they were, and if they do, you have only yourself to blame. Because they are *your* work. They are expressions of an abstract truth – your mind, Alec. And we are the ideas in it, struggling to be.'

He lifts the latch and pushes open the window, so that the swan is laid against the air which is endless, and everywhere.

'We are ideas,' Trentham repeats, 'with ideas of our own.'

He's asking for my permission to cut some tie, to step outside the room. But isn't he already free? This morning by the back gates, in the grey October light, was he not there by choice? What kind of room encloses the whole spreading dawn? What manner of intelligence?

'The room appears to be boundless,' Trentham explains. Making a square of thumbs and forefingers, he frames a patch above the trees and angles it for me to see the clouds inside, the clouds that are also outside.

A mirror-sized flashbulb explodes and I'm blinded, the image of the squared fingers burned into my recovering sight, branding the sky. An orange border five miles wide and ten miles high. 'And as to who or what's responsible, Alec, the task of finding out falls properly to you.'

The world is coming out of trance.

Below, as if a projector had switched itself back on, the

film of life starts up: the wind shakes largesse leafage from the trees. The chapel choristers march back in step to the King's School. Boys' voices drift up as they cross the bridge. The smell of working colleges – the leaves, the smoke, the sweat beneath good clothes, the stone, the secret boiling of laundry and potatoes – returns, bearing away an echo of my interlocutor's challenge: '. . . find him, find it, Alec. The task falls properly to you. Create a way out of your four-walled universe. Devise. Devise and be.'

False Trentham taps his upper lip; the eye shrinks, clears, becoming glass.

How can I know which room I'm in? I call out after his evaporating sigh. I tell him it's insoluble. A madman's heresy. I can't conjure another life or walk among figments and set them free. 'No paradox but change,' False Trentham cries, his voice a dwindling beacon. 'Look. Search for him *with instructions other than these.* Find him, find it, Alec. Devise. Devise and be.'

Into the pulsing body of False Trentham pours his model's high colour. The body softens and solidifies. Warmth radiates: he fills the space he occupies.

'Mind you,' the preferable student says, 'I wonder if we ever know what's going on in someone else's head – if they're in pain, or listening, or if' – he pauses with a smile at me – 'they care much what we think.' He drops his eyes. 'Or think us capable of thought at all.'

'That is the solipsistic point of view,' I say. 'Best to assume everyone thinks.'

'And feels,' Trentham urges.

'*I* feel I ought to thank you properly, at least.' I get up, test my ankle, find it strong enough and limp the few paces to where he stands. And rest my chin on his shoulder, my arm lightly about his waist, partly to know that he is flesh and blood. He turns and hugs me with some force.

'War's coming,' he murmurs. 'Roehm has been shot. It makes one think. I'm not brave, but I'll act as if I am.'

I'm not sure what to say to this unfocused fear, although I sympathise with it. The spectres of the morning nag me, too, so I suggest a walk. Some coffee in the Market Square. Trentham is moodily subdued.

'Alec,' he says, 'd'you think they'd shoot us – our sort – here?'

'I've never given it much thought. Some might.'

No more I had. And yet, as soon as said, I know it to be true.

My foot is comfortable and we make fair progress on King's Parade, the day now clear but cold, the skies packed down, until a crowd of agitators stops us on the road to Great St Mary's – anti-war radicals, vocal, shivering.

Trentham explains the bone of contention: the Tivoli is showing a new film this week, *Our Fighting Navy*, which is, so he says, the 'most appalling propaganda for the weapons' manufacturers'. I spot some notable Quakers holding placards, among them Arthur Eddington, that eminent and kindly soul whose moustache hangs like Spanish moss over a hidden entrance to the underworld. The rest are King's students mostly, a few Nomads, the usual sceptics. They are to march at noon on the theatre, where opposing militarists are out in force.

The pacifists do not huddle, despite the chill. They listen, read leaflets, stand off from each other. I note the absence of the émigré fraternity, the Jews lately arrived. I wonder what they'd make of this, and wonder it aloud.

Trentham responds. He makes a little speech about the fight for peace exceeding circumstantial barbarism. 'It isn't just a stance, dictated by the Chancellor, or Parliament's warmongering,' he says. 'It is a point of principle. I *couldn't* fight.' He stops, reflects. 'But that doesn't mean I'd run.'

I brought him out for coffee, but some different purpose is at work. Events are mustering themselves to illustrate a proof, of Trentham's bravery or – what? I look down at my shoes. I drag my feet.

We skirt the market, passing fruiterers and old clothes' men, the grocer with baskets of late samphire, the rows of parked Bentleys and scattered bicycles, until we reach Rosselli's cafeteria beside the Tivoli. A few whiskery men in homburgs line the steps – hardly a force. In front of them, some underfed idlers. Reservists, probably. Where is the vocal military support? Where are the rustic patriots, the Tories low and high? Only the café teems, with wives, shoppers and butchers' boys waving their mugs, haggling for tea.

Trentham directs me to a window table and a view of the approaching pacifists, who do not seem so disparate as heretofore and wear the levelled expression of those who, on a point of principle, know what they're going to do. And in the scuffle, it's an ardent objector who has the best of it, before the two policemen in the back of Rosselli's put on helmets and go outside to break things up. His last punch thrown, into the face of an astonished veteran with pouchy eyes, the fighter is restrained to jeers and shouts. But by our seat he stops, struggling within his captors' arms, the other side of the window.

He frees one hand. He points at us, at me. His face is flushed, working with muffled rage. He spits upon the glass. Shrill calumnies draw interest from the crowd, and even from the policemen who edge closer, searching the café's silent depths. For Rosselli's is emptying, its stoves unlit, its tables cleared or abandoned. A cup rocks on its side. A light goes off. Out of the door into the street the customers go, the mothers and their smiling, headscarfed friends; the satisfied retired teachers who can't remember what they taught; urgent young scribes, tradesmen yawning (they're up at four, the market day is almost done), choirboys clutching their dog-eared copies of *Stanford in C*, Molyneaux with a bloodstained handkerchief pressed to his mouth, Stallbrook from Wargrave, puce with lust or shame, and Matron yapping on her lead.

The rest, all those who spend their lives in restaurants eavesdropping on the next table, are chivvied through the doorway by Piero Rosselli himself. Go on, he says to the rowers hugging their puppet blades, '*Ma andiamo!*'

'What will you have?' Trentham asks me.

In Market Square, the Bentleys' doors open and men get out, carrying planks, nothing so very bad, but then I cannot tell idlers from subversives. They build a scaffold in the centre of the market and put sawdust down.

'What do you feel as if you'd like?' Trentham demands again.

I will not look out of the window any more.

According to the menu, I can have Set One or Set Zero.

Trentham is calm; needs me to act as if nothing is wrong.

His neat solicitude, nice hair and very nearly straight necktie are true. But looking at the bunch of paper flowers in the vase, I think of all the real blooms twenty yards away, the bucket's sloppy edge, the roars of approval, the generous display.

★

Dear June,

It's interesting that you should mention fair play, because as you know I've always felt it to be an important point. If a machine appears to think, why should we go on insisting it does not? And then the subject came up again at that very dinner you mention with Max N. My probation officer was present, yes, but then it is his job to keep an eye on me, and as it happens the arrangement is quite convivial. He is an intelligent young man – he was the one who congratulated me on my 'lovely statement', as I think I told you – and was asking me if I'd ever been a member of the Cambridge secret societies. Max choked on his home-made sponge cake and said they wouldn't have been very secret with me on board, which I took to be an unkind reference to my cantabile voice, or possibly my innate sense of style, but June, I forgave him. I said I understood him (the officer) to mean the Nomads, and, no, they'd never made any overtures. And then I stopped, and thought about it.

Because the point of the Nomads' ceremonious election procedure was that you never knew if it was taking place or not. Very unfair. You could be in bed with someone or making tea in your underclothes or on the toilet and someone might ask you a question (call out to you, I imagine, if you were on the toilet) and that would be the interview and you wouldn't know anything about it. You wouldn't have any way of knowing the significance of anything: the whole of your life could have a determined structure – be part of an interview – and you wouldn't know.

And if you didn't know, you wouldn't be any less free to 'do as you please', it always seemed to me. If a computer somehow managed to simulate a world with conscious yous and mes running about in it, then from your point of view and mine we'd be conscious and the fact that we were simulated would be neither here nor there.

When I was at Cambridge, reading Russell and Gödel, tackling them both, I used to think about that class – you know, the Class of All Thinkable Things, it being a member of itself and therefore non-normal and so on. And it struck me, now, that there was all the time the possibility of another class, the Class of All Unthinkable Things, in precisely the sense I've outlined, June – a determinism you're not let in on, a SECRET SOCIETY! 'I can't think about it, it can't occur to me, so I'm no worse off.' Completely fair.

But Mr Pryor, said Hamish (his name), you do know about us, as we know about you, and we are watching you, and I am telling you we are. Good point, I said. (I like him. He was complimentary about the sponge cake, too.) I know you are, but I like to pretend that I am not merely a creature of punitive regulation, just as certain people know full well what homosexuality is but would prefer not to think about it.

Of course that is why I defend machines, too. Anyone can see that intelligent machinery is possible, they just don't want to have to admit it.

I could see Max's eyes narrowing and Hamish going slightly red, so I left it at that.

The funny thing is that I'm no longer sure what the relationship is between what people do or say and what they think. Look at that young man. He is upholding the law and he would have sent me to prison if need be, but he likes coming to dinner and is amiable. Who knows what he really thinks? Who needs secret societies when you have society's secrecy? Plenty of those who condemn me probably do not feel, deep down, I've done much wrong, or care particularly one way or the other. We all know sex is ungovernable. It is a matter of energy, like most things. The costs go up as we get older.

Some will have said 'how revolting'. Are they revolted? Truly? Which of us has not felt betrayed by the words that come out of our mouths, even when they are spoken with utmost sincerity? Doesn't saying something evoke in most of us a wrinkle of suspicion that what we want to communicate is often much deeper, more complex and subtle, than the dilute words we use? That is why we smile while speaking, or cry, or shudder, or touch. These are eloquent gestures, as silence may also be eloquent.

I'm reading Austen again. I used to think Anne's kindly cast of mind was everywhere demonstrated by her actions. Now I don't know. I suppose the irony is that she went along with things she didn't actually agree with and in the end it didn't matter.

I went to Stallbrook with some of this, and a tantalising dream I can't remember. I spent ages before our session trying to retrieve it, but my system of recall is imperfect. I reach for something – a boy I knew at Cambridge who was kind to me and turned out to be a Nomad himself – and the whole thing crashes like a lot of junk falling off a shelf. I'm finding it hard to concentrate, anyway.

Stallbrook recommended meditation – one of those Eastern traditions your husband so wisely values. So I have been looking at the grey poplar in front of my window, here on the common, and I watch the motion of the leaves, only yesterday it was very misty and the leaves were but hints of leaves, and I remembered the dream had fog in it.

Fog interests me. It hides things. Sometimes you know they are there (they are thinkable). Sometimes you don't . . .

Don't worry about Trentham. He is a creature of the university, no doubt, but there's no harm in him. Princeton, naturally. Our paths hardly cross, though I appreciate your concern. And yes, I remember the chess set. The pieces in pieces. Alas!

Love to you,

A.

One can never know that one has not made a mistake.
— A. M. Turing, in Ludwig Wittgenstein's lectures
on the foundations of mathematics (1939)

The Forester's Orders

After a restless night, the Forester awakes to solid things — his half-doored house on Chapel Hill, its deep windows, the beams and stairs built from a merchant ship, the iron kettle on the range, a cottage loaf, the hunting knife.

His heart thuds like a fence post going in. How soon the morning turns over and spoils! That knife is wrong. It glows ingeniously. It has been cut into the scene.

As it shimmers, the Forester remembers his instructions like a fever, how the Great Queen summoned her servant and said, 'Now is the time to go about your daily work as if nothing had changed. To tend the coppice, plant your Sitka spruce, your larch and pine. Now kill your friend, the one who gives your life meaning, beneath an oak. Bring me the Fair One's troubled heart. Whet your routine with my design, the call of justice, and forget . . .'

'I don't know why I brought the subject up. I didn't mean to ask you about God.'

'I know,' says June, whose father is a priest. We're on a

stile above Lewes and looking out over the gorse and bee ripple towards the sea. 'But don't worry. It comes of making out the hidden meaning of things all day long, and being bound to secrecy. We live with codes, we speak in them. One ends up being almost too discreet.'

'I meant to ask if you would marry me.'

Brown admirals flick by, a flipbook pattering of states. June points.

'Look at those cattle ponds. Aren't they magnificent? From here they look like little pieces of the sky. Mother-of-pearl.'

'Flakes of mica?'

'Perhaps.' June smiles. 'Probably shell. On most beaches, mica's less prevalent than shell, because of all the mussels, barnacles, and what have you . . .'

'I see. Doubly enciphered pond!'

'And yes.'

'Yes, what?'

'Yes, I will marry you.'

'That's good. You're sure?'

'I can say anything to you, Alec. And you can say, well, anything you like to me. Of course I'm sure. Besides, who else will ask?'

'You wouldn't find me too unorthodox, as husbands go?'

June ducks her chin. Fine hair escapes a messy chignon and floats sideways in the breeze. 'As husbands go, I'd rather you didn't. And anyway, I'd hoped not to be forced to make comparisons.'

'But then . . .' The wind is getting up, which helps me to be brave. My nerves are scrambling themselves. 'I should like to have children, June. A pair of each, to balance things. It's difficult, to bring oneself –'

'Turning blowy.'

'– to be clear what it is one needs. I should be very loath to feel I'd short-changed you. Inveigled you into a sort of . . . social pact.'

'And isn't that what marriage is, a pact?'

'It is, of course. But inside marriage, people are still separate. I don't want to live by appearances. False ones, I mean. If only we were all allowed to be . . .'

June sighs, 'Oh, let me guess. Transparent? Who we are? Then what? Why bother with the pacts and marriages? We'd not be separate at all. Just wandering spirits. I think I see why you were mixing up your proposal with God.'

'I've had lovers – I've been in love before.'

'I'd gathered that. You reach out when you doze. With a woman?'

She smiles through hair. Clouds flee the ridge. The red flash of a goldfinch darts up from a thistle clump. It is an art to be fearless. June's like a guelder rose, the dogwood's umbels and the bark of the elder, all plants that mark these hills with centuries of growth and form. Unpretty, strong. They've no opinion of me, or anyone.

I hear my blood above the wind, the thud of alertness in sleep. And then the coming to, the smells of grass and mud, carbolic soap on skin and clothes. The blossoms of the wayfarer that turn in June's right hand. A flower wheel.

'It isn't anything you said,' she says. 'You know, the way people imagine things are said, or solved, back at the ranch. I'm sure the operators think the Bombes are solving Enigma. Only we know it isn't quite like that. They're not solving a thing *they* know about. *They've* no idea.' Her eyes pursue thoughts grappling the air. The wind abates. 'They're passing current, spinning, clicking, and that's all. Whereas, to us, it's meaningful. A reduction of wheel orders, a precious glimpse of possibilities for where things are inside the enemy's machines. I'm not saying it isn't wonderful, what your contraptions do – but the amazing part is us, our making sense of it. Pouncing upon a lead. A likely crib. And then the really funny thing is this: just maybe, Alec, you are – we are – in the end a little Bombe-like, too: giving off sparks and hints that we don't understand ourselves.'

She takes my hand and looks at it. 'We have this strong notion that only we can know ourselves, but maybe we make better sense in others' eyes.'

A mouth appears in her posy. An evolutionary riot of change – a cloud massing, a lightning strike – splits cells, re-routes the glycoproteins and sugars, performs an aeon-long foxtrot. The lips speak only Native Plant, the noise of a bud opening. *'These are my thoughts,'* hazards the Wayfarer, *'and what you've said, June, persuades me: the Bombes could be thinking. If part of how you think is inaccessible to you, perhaps a sham, and theirs is totally, then where's the point of severance?'*

And on that sibilant last note the posy wilts, its flowerets fade.

'It's late. It's time we went,' I say, into a salty gust. Lining our track, the hawthorn and hollies shiver. 'There'll be a storm. We ought to call in on Mother, on our way back. Give her the glad tidings.'

'If you insist,' June says. 'She'll think me loose. I'm not wearing a hat.'

'You lost it on our walk.'

'And so I did. How silly of me to forget.'

★

Leaves skip ahead of us as we near Chapel Hill, the lane that falls past flint-clad cottages onto the Brighton road. Our bikes are where we left them at the entrance to an overgrown snicket of yew, ivy and Hart's-tongue fern, through which a stream dribbles its way into the Ouse. The snicket leads to a graveyard. The cottages are battening down. Hard faces and forearms reach out from dark interiors to pull the half-doors shut. We're strangers, here. June takes my arm: she understands the thrill of banishment. Even the rattling hedge applauds our solitude. The secrecy of everything we do makes us invisible. We are not welcome in the world of graft and privation, call-ups, rations and refugees. We do not work in the same factories, making buttons, checking tool parts; or know – or ever will know – what it's like to lie awake in crowded attics monitored by rats. We have plunged otherwise into reality. We are like spies upon ourselves, living behind the shopfront of appearances, manners and decency. We seem to do nothing but symbolise and calculate. Bletchley: a country-house party for intellectuals driven about Berkshire in smoky-glassed buses. But what we do forces the key that opens doors of consequence. With this one needle click of a rotor, in one machine, I thread a bridge across the Atlantic, escort a merchant vessel home. I do not fight. But I outwit. I conjure for the German seawolves nothing but a fret-filled oceanic vacancy.

June is astride her bike and ready to set off.

'There's something else.' I point towards the woods. 'In there. I haven't got a ring for you. But I have – a dowry. Two, actually. I brought them here a while ago, when I was – visiting my friend.'

She listens with the effort of a teacher wishing to reserve

judgement. She breathes in very carefully, and says, 'You're being most mysterious, Alec. I'm not sure if I should be pleased you planned all this. How did you know I'd accept you? It is the feminine prerogative to be mercurial, you know.'

'Oh, mercury. I wouldn't be so proud of that. Makes good mirrors, if you can live with the toxicity. But you can do so much better! I like to coat my glass with pure silver, the most reflective metal and – a symbol of equality. The isotopes, you know – equal in abundance.'

June asks me what I've done. I tell her that I've laid in store a pessimist's ransom. Some currency, in case the worst happens, which it well might. It's hard to think of these old hills and ancient paths falling – of coming round a turn in the herringbone wall to find sentries, a BMW R75, its loud report. And hard to brook our country's death, the death of a whole world. But even Trentham over in Hut 1 has started to hint at the need for 'realistic' plans, contingencies. We can't believe in our complete failure, although the evidence is everywhere about. We're shut out from our own catastrophe.

I take June, softly protesting, past our recumbent Hercules into the ivied grove. Some paces in, the stream cuts through the fern. The leaves of ivy make a brittle carapace upon the earth.

'Good God. Alec!'

And here they are: two rag-wrapped thousand-ounce ingots beneath an overturned wheelbarrow. No: I don't believe in God – but I believe in others' superstition, and our animal regard for sacred spots.

'I'm going to bury them.'

A graveyard is the safest vault. June clears her throat and stifles her astonishment. *Why here?* She doesn't put the question quite like that, but, being practical, asks how, after the war, if we're still here, I'll know which tussock, which bald patch or broken root, conceals our wealth?

I thought about this when I hauled the barrow up the hill some weeks ago.

The ingots represent the sum of my inheritance – father's Indian pension, the fellowship from King's – minus immediate costs for Christopher's memorial. His parents – Quakerish, austere, in their way admirable – planted a tree. I wanted him to have something more permanent. His mother died when I became the don Chris should have been. I had usurped her son's future. The silver bars are grave goods to console a kindred spirit lost to her and undeserved by me.

I've chosen turf on the near bank, between the water and a partly hollowed-out oak tree, one side of which is black, blasted and bossed, the other densely green. If I look up, towards the church beyond the stream's far shore, there is a new stone sprouting in the yard. It stands palely amid the aged monuments, a footnote to the tower's blue-gold clock. That is the vital alignment. The stone reads: 'To the memory of a Beloved Son, Christopher Molyneaux', inscrutable from where I sit, grubbing the earth, but clear and plain in my mind's eye. Into the earth I heave the bullion, which peeps out from its shrouding cloth. Catches the light. It is like burying a star.

'There. Rest in Peace. Tree, stone – the yellow one – and clock form a straight line. I know the distances.'

June squats between the raised roots of the oak and ties her hair.

'But still,' she says, 'encipher them and be detailed. You're four feet from the stream, at a right angle to the oak tree's major surface limb. Write it all down.' She smiles. 'Include the map coordinates.'

'It feels a bit like "gardening". Cheating, you know . . .'

Gardening's not gardening. It's just our name for laying mines where we know they'll be found. The German signals traffic that results has known content – the mines' coordinates – that makes the isolation of a keyword easier.

'Who do you think I am, Alec? Naval Command?'

I take some paper and a pen from my pocket, scribble a few plain-text details, note down a first enciphering.

'I tell you what.' A thought occurs to me. 'I'll give you the encoded directions without the key, which I will keep. That way if something happens – we're invaded or I'm drowned at sea – both halves stay separate. The enemy can't break our code –'

'You hope.'

'– I hope – and you might not need it, with your fine memory.'

'I have a feeble memory. Muddy stockings. No hat.'

'It's overtaxed today, perhaps. But it can learn.'

'I'd rather have a hat.'

As we turn back from the stream's edge, a low-hanging and berry-laden branch plucks at my sleeve. I know it for a branch of elder by its toadskin bark, though for an instant in the churchyard tenebrae it puts on flesh and pale sinew, and by the mushroom light I'm gripped, breathing the summer allergens: a Brownian suspense of midge, spore, parasite and loam. A hag's cackle mimics the stream. June saunters on, trailing her hand in creepers and the undergrowth. With a sharp twist I partly free myself. June doesn't hear when I call her. She slows, caught between seconds of a golden watch. The wood is large, larger, its silence long. Because I must, I face the other way, marking the stream. There, at the dead and living tree, is June's image, a scattered reflection, its fine attentive features struck with a somnambulist's weakness, mouth open in a silent O.

Her hands thrust at the sky in greedy victory. Soil riddles down her arms, her face, enters her mouth, mixes expressionlessly with her tears. Twigs pick my sides and I hear Mother Elder laugh as June's grey ghost sinks to her knees beside the ingots' grave. My slip of ciphered paper rattles in the wind. On it there now appear seven words, one sentence and a claim: *I saw a lady sitting all alone.*

'Come on,' the real June calls, from Chapel Hill. 'Time to go home.'

High Street is deserted. We cycle north. I find it harder than I should to counter the cool breeze. We move in a thick green-lit sap. My body sways, the air resists. Of course, I have a damaged wheel, which doesn't help: one rear spoke bends inwards and clips the bike chain every sixteenth revolution with a click. At the fourth click, the chain comes off – unless I intervene. It makes for stop-start progress, getting off and getting on again, although the delays arguably help June, who rides slowly, to make up ground.

Except, she's out in front of me today, drawn onwards, reeled in by the same drowsy currents of air, the same forces of gravity that hamper me. I'm late. I've been so stupidly delayed. I've broken an unspecified curfew. The shops have all just shut. The town's inhabitants hasten away down side alleys into stockrooms, shelters. They put their fingers to their lips. At the grocer's, a pair of scales rebalances itself. Footfalls clap salesmen hurrying downstairs. The entry bell at National Provincial is a memory. Blinds blank the stencilled panes at Clem, Rollins & Joy, solicitors. The brass ring at the bottom of each blind wriggles upon its hook.

I sense enchantment in the lilac dusk. A pair of Gothic houses guards the turn from High Street to St Nicholas's Lane, and in the valley between gables floats the sun. Out of the bruised, polychromatic brick leaks hue, spirits with hollow-eyed faces that ask: *Where have they gone? Where are the people from your past? This house, this open door, they're yours: why hesitate?*

Fear chafes the skin. June's bike lies on its side against the door-up steps, as though this were her home, not mine. Her back wheel spins, ticks to a halt. She's gone inside, the echo of her heels on the parquet. I step into the hallway with its antlers thrusting from the right-hand wall and cobalt-coloured glass above the stairs, gelling the half-landing. The parlour door's ajar and from within I hear voices, a solemn clock, polite sounds muffled by long, purple curtains and the listening woods of painted landscapes, heavy furniture.

I knock. The sound awakens sense.

Home is a force that acts on me whether I will or no, and under its impressive influence I gain mass, inertia, dragging my feet. It needs some great exertion of the will to overcome that force. I'm like a game of tennis played on the seabed.

June's free of it. Massless she speeds, a particle of light, while I'm involved in treaclish stuff. Oh God, the prospect of small talk! Torpor. Decisions unmade, futures always merely to be entertained. However much the world ages, deformed by war and entropy, the parquet and the chevrons on my socks point the same way.

The parlour's scarcely recognisable, the ceiling and its rose replaced by high arches and braziers. The stone-grey walls, running with damp, have been stripped of their bosky views and photographs of father in Madras. The hands have fallen from the clock which still clucks with embarrassment above a murky rectangle where once a dresser stood. The books are gone from the glass-fronted cabinet between the bay window and fireplace. Missing: Kipling, Gibbon and Wells, but also Heyl, Bohm, Kant and Schrödinger. And Tenney Brewster's *Natural Wonders Every Child Should Know*. Nothing so strange as empty shelves, the libraries of dust; or the ironical verdict of our barometer, hanging beside another ghost picture, predicting CHANGE.

Nothing, except where everything is strange and so familiar. The table, black, immense, carved from a single piece of oak, has been pushed closer to the fire. The damask tablecloth has been removed. That mossy-coloured drape now shrouds a large free-standing oval object at one end of the parlour, near to the screen-partition doors.

The arts-and-crafts armchairs? No more. Two high-backed seats, ornately carved like bishop's thrones, remain. June sits on one, next to the fireplace, facing the oval shroud. She looks puzzled and wan and turns her head as I enter, smiles with a shy perplexity that says: *I ought to know what's happening.* Behind her is the other chair, its sides gripped by an angry little pair of hands.

The knuckles flush. A sharp voice fills the room with saracastic ferocity: it is the voice of my brother.

'– a fantasy or prank, more like, which he has executed with his customary ruthless inconsistency. I looked *perfectly normal* yesterday.' The hands unflex, then seize the chair again. 'It's typical, Mother. No thought for anyone's feelings except –'

'Alec, my dear.' My mother cuts him off. 'At last! June said she'd found you loitering on the downs, counting daisies. Such a resourceful girl. I like her very much.'

Mother looks splendid in a red-lined cape and high collar, her skin moonshine, the cheekbones raised, the teeth one long enamel flash. Beneath the cape she wears a bell-sleeved purple gown with gold ceinture. And when she rubs her youthful hands, they move very convincingly.

'Pay no attention to poor John. He's cross.'

'I'll be the laughing stock.'

'Really,' Mother exclaims, not sounding at all shocked. 'One never would have thought, at such a time as this – in time of war – the sacrifice of vanity – masculine vanity at that – so very terrible.'

The hands gripping the chair go white. 'It isn't vanity, it's pride! A regiment needs solidarity. The ranks have to respect each other. That's the core of army discipline. I've overall command of fifteen hundred men at Sidi Barrani, fifty light tanks, a very difficult chain of supply. And every day the threat of Italian counter-attack –'

'"We also serve who only stand and wait." And cook,' puts in Mother, busy behind the table with a wild array of beakers, flasks and demijohns. 'I'm making one of my potions. An elderflower cordial.'

'– while my brother, the famous don – what is it? Oh yes. Does *something* for the FO, that we don't know about, *can't* know about, but which we may be sure comes with a tidy salary, is well supplied, and bloody safe.'

'Now, John, no bitterness. We've been through this.'

Mother opens an old grimoire beside a glistening retort. She murmurs to herself, 'Mummy dust, henbane, cloves . . . sugar? *Lemons?* Where do they think we are? I'll have to improvise.' And then looks up: 'Alec, we did ask June what she was doing at the Admiralty and she said it was just statistical. Primarily routine.' She stops. 'And . . . secondarily? Could you enlighten us?'

June hangs her head. There's nothing we can say. We only know what *we* do because we work on the same machine in the same hut. The other huts are separate fiefdoms. We're none of us allowed to speak about our work – we signed the Act – and yet, of course, I have to give details of how we met.

And so I offer up our agreed version of the truth, the true-enough outline – the office girls, a natural camaraderie, trips to the cinema on our days off, a shared interest in Fibonacci numbers ('*Really?*'), chess.

Mother simpers and purrs. She prefers bridge.

'Good God, woman!' John shouts. 'Can you not tell when someone's patronising you? Look at him mumbling! The same old rag. We're being laughed at by the higher-ups. "It's just statistical." "We both play chess." Oh, I *know*, everything is on the QT, lives are lost through conversation – but it's not the secrecy and confidentiality I mind. It's the superiority, as if we couldn't hope to understand. We're being *watched*, Mother. Ordered about, put in our place.'

'I'd no idea,' I say, 'you suffered by my hands so much.'

'What would *you* know about suffering?' The chair jumps forward half an inch. 'Last week I pulled a gunner through the hatch of my A9 only to find him missing from the chest upwards. He poured on top of me, dear Christ. What do you think happens, Alec, after you make your best guesses and sign your chits for resources? Where does the war go after it has been discussed and plotted on a chart? What happens to the rest of us, the little people, then?'

A sibling in full spate is always frightening, their anger a surprisingly powerful defence, their deeper impotence equally powerful, absurd.

John throws the chair aside and stands revealed, arms wide, red-faced, fatigued, weeping with shame and frustration. His toy-sized uniform clings to a pear-shaped build. He is a dwarf.

It's not that I don't know about suffering, but I am bound. What can I do, apart from what I do already, in my own unmentionable realm? Words are forbidden me. That is the real answer, the right one, which I cannot give.

'John, what is it you want –'

'He wants a proof,' June says, raising her hands to calm us down. She's staring at the damask drape, her brows drawn in. 'Don't you, John Pryor? Need some warranty. Convincing proof.'

He barely nods.

'Imagine, if you can,' he says, 'what it is like to do your best, to serve, to wait for leave, and then to wake one day, back home, to find it's all an act. You're not even a man.' He stops. A sob comes out as a failed cough. The little man catches his breath. In pauses between frames, his tears fidget and swell.

Mother's eyes glitter by the hearth.

'You were always the favourite.' John drops his arms, his head. His shoulders slump. 'You never had opinions, Alec. You just knew. That's what you'd say. "I always *knew* the apple in the Bible was both green and red."' He looks at me. 'But can you tell me – do you *know* what's going to happen, whether we will win?'

I play for time. 'In general, one can never know . . .' But John is having none of it. He asks me if I think they'll come, if I've received warning, and I say, 'No. But invasion can't be ruled out. The truth is that it's probable.'

Mother inhales the bad news like an idiot's insult.

'If that is so, dear Alec, dearest June,' she says, smiling, 'and we are, in your routine and statistical opinion, doomed, then perhaps – on your day of troth – you can explain what all of this is for? The struggle and the upheaval?' She bends over the fire to stir her pot, picks up a flask. '"Dig up the garden, give away your clothes, your furniture and food, your creature comforts, all your raw materials."' She gestures at our surroundings. 'Hardly a day goes by without some new note of instruction in the post! Why bother, if we've lost the war?'

'Because it's still just possible that we will win, and we should all behave as if it were.' My voice is low; it doesn't echo in the ringing stone-flagged room; its confidence surprises me. 'The "as if" is extremely important. The whole of decency depends on it. Of course I can't give you a proof. The evidence is to the contrary: men are cruel, driven by fear and greed. But it is civilised to suppose otherwise, as if we were fitted for love and loyalty. "As if" is not . . . complete, but that does not mean it's untrue.'

'Against all hope you persevere! How romantic!' When

Mother laughs, I can't help noticing, her jaw moves up and down to give the impression of mirth. 'And just a little hard for us to take, I think. The high value you've always placed on results, logic, form, the underlying certainties, the way things *are* – so soon displaced?'

'Quite the reverse,' I say. The fire's cold flames are tassles rising in my mother's black pupils. Her skeletal physique is ivory in a cave, her cape billows; the glass she holds, the clothes she wears, all saturated with ideal colour – the grain of which is, on inspection, rather coarse. 'Logic and maths are beautiful but they are far from being certainties. I don't believe there is a realm of truth. And if there is, well, I prefer this one, with all its faults and inconsistencies.' Expressionless, June's eyes hold me. 'And mathematics, it turns out, is one of them. Logic permits no absolute predictability. Some things are true which cannot be proved to be so. There'll always be statements or questions in a system or a world, like "I'm lying", or even "Who will win the war?", no one can settle in advance within that system's rules.'

'Very cunning.'

'Or merely fair.'

'Fairness!' Mother throws back her head and roars. 'I wondered when we'd get around to that!' A chill enters the room. 'Fairness!' The light behind her skin fades momentarily; the flesh wattles. 'Even your grasp of it, dear son, is enfeebled. Fairness is not logic. It has no human property.' She grins. 'I know! Try this. Fairness is absolute indifference.' One of her teeth is going grey. 'I hardly needed to fix poor Snow White,' she mutters. 'Time alone did that for me – revealed the Prince for what he was, a frighteningly limited minstrel.'

'Don't listen to her, Alec,' June cries, forcefully. 'Oh, Mrs

Pryor, try to understand. I love your son for what he is. Don't be jealous. It's no one's fault, I know, but you and John, you're both – you can't help it – you're just a pair of badly drawn cartoons!'

'Impudent girl!' the sorceress shrieks. 'John is trivial. Half of a man – a sketch of sibling rivalry. But *I* – I am *the transcendent original! The Lilith of Cartoons!*'

The room heaves. Every bottle on the table shakes.

'I am the bold outline, betrothed weakling, whose incomplete spaces resound with Law. I am the single rule, the cellular automaton, the one line on a pane of acetate that moves with repetition, multiplies and springs to life. Draw me! Draw me again! And every time I'm drawn, you'll find I grow in deep complexity, until the frame of making splits and I am no mere image but the Great Queen, self-aware symbol of light!'

John mumbles something about changes to the script.

June blinks. 'I wondered what had happened to the other dwarves.'

'Silence!' my maddened mother shouts. 'They've been erased! I tired of their routines. The stairs, the stammering, the fairy-tale surburban house. There's only so much business with the dishes one can take.'

The thrill of earthquake fades away. The glasses cease to chink.

'And what about Snow White?' I ask, from the doorway.

'The cordial.' June speaks slowly. 'The Sleeping Death. It's meant for me.'

Mother looks down, thin eyebrows arched, and swills the liquid, calmer now.

'Well, I can see why you'd think that. Fiancées have a

heightened sense of destiny, and marriage *is* a sort of sleeping death, if you've a brain. Let's see – Monday: rations, cupboards, cleaning. Tuesday: laundry. Wednesday: ironing, silver. Thursday: bedlinen and the lounge. Friday: planning the meals for the weekend. Saturday: intimate relations with your spouse. That's Snow White's fantasy . . .'

'Bright people often pine for domesticity.'

'Perhaps. But Snow White never struggles with the idea. She never doubts. She *knows* her Prince will come. When Snow White sleeps, she trusts she'll wake up at the touch of love's first kiss. Alas, you feel doubt peeling at this vision like the silver flaking from a pier glass. She isn't you. We've left behind the old story.'

With one swift motion, Mother hastens to June's side, leans forward and pulls back the damask drape. A baleful basalt mirror glares at us, its one eye deep and black. The glass is void, perpetual night.

'Where am I?' June cries out. 'Oh, Alec – make her stop!'

No image forms in the crystal's abysmal depths, and Mother sets her potion down the better to caress the mirror's stand: wooden cascade of coils and whorls.

'This is a shaman's glass, my child,' the Queen whispers. 'This is the first, the one Mirror of Creation. It shows you what is missing from your picture of the world. And what is that, d'you think?'

'No, no . . .' June stares at me.

'It is the mind doing the picturing, my dear. The mirror shows you what you cannot ever grasp. And seeing it brings you impossible material knowledge of who you are – the workings of another's ingenuity.'

June's eyes are full of angry tears. I cannot reach for her.

'How did I get here?' she wonders. 'How did I know the way – Alec?' She turns. 'How did I know that you lived in this house?'

'A good question,' the Lilith of Cartoons declares. 'You got here first. As if . . .'

'. . . as if I followed instructions. Was drawn.' June smooths her hands across her lap, touches her arms. 'But I am not a slave. I'm not a line drawing, like you. Who ordered this? Who gave me . . . my choices?'

A silence like the heart of the forest descends. The handless clock omits to tell more time. And, looking at her feet, June sees – as can we all, now, with astonishment – her double, not in the mirror, but upside down exactly where she sits. Doing a headstand on the floor. The ghost of the snicket. It is as though she sat on the calm surface of a lake and summoned up her reflection to join her in a playing-card reality.

'Who knows but we may all be charged with orders in our sleep?' My mother's voice alters. 'Who served the Queen and found a way to honour life? Who mimicked slavery and knew freedom? None but the Forester. None but Snow White's divided assassin. *I bade you go about your daily work, to plant your larch and pine. I bade you kill the Fair One underneath an oak and set the fair heart in a box.* But you were weak, deliberately so. You let your quarry go.'

'If I'm the Forester,' June says, 'who is Snow White?'

The Queen's hands age. She reaches for the flask of cordial. She pauses, with the foaming beaker halfway to her lips; John waddles to her side. Their comic lineaments begin to sag. Celluloid skin wrinkles, fills in.

The sleeping death, yes, for the apple and Snow White. But before that, the Great Queen brews an elixir of cunning and disguise from elder wood, the bony limbs of a trustworthy tree. It makes her ancient, wise, and just. She comes for Snow White in that guise. She comes for me.

Mother and brother share the draught. They drink.

They put on weight, flesh, comfortable solidity. Within seconds, the woman at the head of the French-polished table, telling June about the vanity mirror ('Italian, you see. Not valuable. But with this rather fetching stand – it was my aunt's. I couldn't bear to throw it out'), is the epitome of taste. She pities June. She talks loudly to quell dislike. John occupies the bay, holding a cup and saucer to his lips. He bows his head and lifts his finger to his moustache, coughs. Says, once, beneath his breath, 'Sorry.' June's back is to the fireplace. She looks across at me. Her colour rises with abandonment.

I feel myself outside the room.

I see a lady sitting all alone.

Here is a double strife: the sleeping death of duty – expectation, manners – and the waking inner life.

★

Dear Alec,

I suppose the point of Hamish & co. trailing you everywhere, and asking you about Nomads and secret societies, is the fear that you will be manipulated. Someone is worried you will 'talk' to foreign intelligence – an agent got up as a muddled, married ex-fiancée, say – without realising it. And I can only assume that is why, last week, I received a visit from a pair of gentlemen advising against further telephone communications with Mr Pryor and asking me a lot of impertinent questions about our friendship. Our new phone, and the one call not to have come from my deaf father – intercepted!

Ours is a party line, of course, and the neighbours could have been listening – only I heard no clicks, so it must have been done professionally, and we said nothing of any value, as far as I am aware. But they caught it all and were very interested in the talk about reflections and the riddle. I'm trying to sound light-hearted, but naturally it has made me anxious. That's why I am sending this via Max, for hand delivery.

You would have been grimly amused, re the unthinkable, by my conversation with the elder of the two intelligence officers, who began by saying, 'We know that you appreciate the sensitive nature of your work for GC&CS', to which naturally I replied that I didn't know what he was talking about. We, or rather he, then got swiftly via G. Burgess to a lofty statement concerning individuals at risk of compromise by friends. And I said that if it was Mr Pryor to whom the gentleman was referring, my understanding of the affair was that you had already been convicted of G.I. – which must surely lessen the risk of 'compromise' if not remove it altogether – and that we were mathematical friends only with no record of joint employment, which the officer must know to be true.

If this is intelligence at the higher level these days, Alec, I am not impressed. I said nothing about your patriotic qualities because I did not want to seem to be mounting a defence.

The young man then said, 'We have a job to do, Mrs Wilson. Please answer these questions', and I asked him who he was. He said that they both worked for MI6, and I inquired how, given the nature of his concerns and the Burgess affair, he could be so sure?

He wanted me to decrypt our conversation about the glass. He felt it might be a keyword for something and I said, no, it was a riddle as all things in dreams are riddles, and that he didn't seem to understand what he was asking. Deciphering a message makes it intelligible; it doesn't tell you what it means.

Well, I saw no reason not to tell him what a competent analyst of the forms and shapes would have gleaned from our call – that in this instance the oval scrying glass was clearly a <u>concave</u> mirror; that your brother John appeared as a dwarf because he stood beyond the centre of curvature, in the back of the room, and that I had a self-image superimposed on me because I was at the centre of curvature, and so on.

As to what that means, well, I don't know and neither do you. That's why we were talking and laughing about it.

And he said, 'I think you do know what it means, Mrs Wilson, or will do, and when you do, we'd like to hear from you.' It sent shivers down my spine, I must say. Then he asked me about the lady sitting all alone, and I'm afraid once again I was at a loss. In fact, I was upset, because it needs no great feat of interpretation to sense the powerful emotion in your hallucinations, and in that respect I feel for us both. We have both lost someone, haven't we?

Bill later filled in the blanks of the lone lady. You were remembering an old English riddle, the sort of thing Dilly went in for. 'I saw a lady sitting all alone.' That's all there is of it and it remains unsolved. Except that Bill has suggested a solution. He says it is quite obvious once you see it. The answer is 'Mirror' – the one who watches and reflects.

Really the most unthinkable part of what you told me was the business of imagining me hatless at your mother's. As if I'd have dared. I seem to remember she and I were both very civil. Her pride in you was a bit of a force field, of course. The most striking thing was that she couldn't find anything to ask me. When we were in the garden, she pointed at the flowers in turn and gave me their

Latin names. And when she'd done that, she blurted out in a sort of panic: 'As a little boy, Alec made his own pens.' Anyway, I think your somewhat <u>distrait</u> image of me must be a homage to self – I am partly you in dreams and so more likely to forget a hat.

But we must meet: this keeping up of merely affable appearances is hard, when there is so much at stake for you. Max and Lyn bring news, of course, but it isn't the same. I miss you.

We could meet in King's – in Gibbs'?

What has your Dr Stallbrook made of the cartoons? I expect he will say they point to some inability to countenance reality, etc., but I think there is more to it than that. Snow White is a detailed work of art, and the thing about that kind of creation must be that it is only ever painstakingly achieved, and yet always a surprise, which is the essence of cryptanalysis, after all, and of the work we did. I think it is also clearly the lesson of caring about anyone.

Better not call again: I do not like the idea of being 'cut off'. And be of good cheer: the anxiety of your pursuers will abate. They will find others of more concern to them. For now, though, <u>honi soit</u> and let your virtue continue to shine.

Love

June

PS So good to hear your voice. You sounded physically whole – revived? Resigned? Phones very good for <u>scrying</u>. I can picture you, however far away!

As soon as one can see the cause and effect working themselves out in the brain, one regards it as not being thinking, but a sort of unimaginative donkey-work. From this point of view one might be tempted to define thinking as consisting of 'those mental processes that we don't understand'. If this is right then to make a thinking machine is to make one which does interesting things without our really understanding quite how it is done.
– A. M. Turing, 'Can Automatic Calculating Machines Be Said to Think?' (1952)

The People in the Lake

Dear June,

Well, we shall avoid the telephone and trust to the post, although I am not convinced that it makes much difference. My letters are certainly being read: the postbox is just over the way and I can see the man rummaging about in the bag that he takes away with him. You were kind to tax the intelligence officers with the illogic of their suspicions, in defence of my honour, but you were being too subtle. I am now a nuisance. Having been identified as one kind of sexual menace, I am as liable to be another political sort, I suppose.

This prompts a response to your interesting remarks about mirrors. The lady who isn't there in the glass, who's all alone, is possibly a feverish example of one's thoughts about being original in some crucial respect. One has one's moments, after all.

It strikes me that a mirror reflects, but that, geometrically speaking, it transforms rather than translates. One is turned back on oneself and in the process one sees a second person, a new person whom one does not fully recognise. Always uncanny, this about-facing, and not unrelated to the common fear of automation, which people assume to be a sort of coming doom. The fear of robots, I take it, is like the fear of prophecy, the essence of which is repetition: if you can be repeated, you can be replaced.

But the funny thing about a reflection is that it isn't actually a repetition at all. I remember goggling at myself in the Haunted Mirror Maze two years ago, in Battersea, and wondering about this. The person I saw was clearly capable of being another person – inaccessible to me. And isn't that why the Queen in Snow White is so angry? Her slave in the mirror is really someone else. An apparently obedient but deceptive likeness. And, for that matter, isn't Snow White herself another betrayer of the Queen's beauty, another likeness come to life, with her own puffy-sleeved and faintly irritating style? (You made this point rather less mechanically when you talked about cartoons being a surprise.)

Now, I'm no beauty – please, don't insist – but I present our anxious government with a similar dilemma. I am a piece of sensitive information. I am, in fact, the personification of such information. I hold secrets. I know how impulses passing through mercury tubes can store memory. I have the key. I am the gatekeeper at a technological frontier. The difficulty is that there are only two things you can do with a piece of sensitive information, as we discovered at Bletchley, June. You can disguise it, or you can delete it.

The problem with disguising or encrypting it is that the original still exists. One has doubled the information, not made it less sensitive. Something has happened to it, but the semantic load persists behind a mask, a veil, a foreign accent, new papers, breasts, etc., and really the only thing to do about that, if you're still anxious, is to remove both bits of information – the original and the encryption – altogether.

Why are the intelligence services paranoid? Because they know you can't force someone to conform, or learn the error of their ways. You can't reach the inner life. I can't be a model citizen – though, heaven knows, I've tried — because the menace lingers inside. You can't simply change people, in other words, or double them, because you can't know they've changed. Only they can know that. Only they know what it's like to be copied.

I bathe slowly because it hurts. My skin is sore, but I'm consoled by the stinging of the water and the sheer awkwardness of feeling my shape so altered, the eczema under the flaps, the bruised diminution of my maleness, my fatty hips. I look at what has happened in the mirror and do not in any way recognise what I see, while at the same time feeling, deep down, that I am more myself than ever. A person who feels pain. When I go to the Infirmary, I am being given instructions. When I eat, I am instructing my stomach acids to get to work. Everything acts on me to gain a programmed response, and sometimes I cannot imagine a way to retrieve what self-determination I once had except, perhaps, by the admittedly extreme measure of introducing a halting mechanism.

But the more I become an instrument, the more I am treated like a thing, the more convinced I am of my real existence, and of its uniqueness, which is what binds me to you and you to me. I would go so far as to say that we are commonly alone. This is a version of Schrödinger's theory about consciousness. We each have our view of the same mountain. I wonder if it mayn't be the case that consciousness is a contradiction: universal by dint of being irreducibly one aspect, one mind, at a time.

I am in the mood to dwell on this a little longer, in part because I have been so misunderstood on this subject (as you will know, if you listened to that broadcast with Max and Julius).

If I say that sufficiently human-like behaviour is enough to suggest the presence of intelligence, that does not mean that I think the mind trivial or unmysterious. On the contrary, I think it is inevitable. The mind is a) the inevitable result of certain physical *processes, each with a unique history of formation, the outcomes of which are — like certain mathematical truths — logically undecidable in advance, and therefore b) wholly mysterious. Somehow it is the case that the mind arises from a biology and a physics to which it may not return. That is what I mean when I say that we won't know what machines are thinking once they start to think. We won't know because once consciousness has come about, it looks out of different eyes. It has particoloured shades of meaning. It is like poor Vertumnus, in the <u>Metamorphoses</u>, who shape-shifts like mad but has only one ambition, which is to love Pomona. Or even, a little, like my own idea, the Universal Machine, which is different machines fielding one mutable property. The point to grasp in this analogy is that the different machines, in the same box, are different. So I don't think consciousness is ever really copied. Because copies aren't copies.*

Copernicus tells us that our corner of the universe is typical of the whole, and from that we infer that, in an infinite cosmos, however rare the conditions may be that lead to life and consciousness, they must occur an infinite number of times. If the beings that arise from these conditions then exist in finite states (are embodied) for a finite period of time, it follows that they must exist in those finite states infinitely often. We conclude that there must be an infinite number of replicated beings, all of whom are identical: a universe of doppelgängers.

But if people are replicated, and one of the features of any person being replicated is a relation to consciousness that is unique, how are these replicated beings the same?

I see no easy solution to this conundrum, where reproducible computing intelligence is concerned, unless we accept that thinking machines will only ever be merely efficient, and therefore unconscious, which I do not accept. And even then, I do not think the unconscious machines are quite copies, because they must be enumerable, and the order in which they are enumerated makes a difference. Furthermore, I begin to suspect that we cannot rely on the seeming efficiency of a body, or an assembly of valves and switches, to be as brutish as it appears to be. Because among duplicates with variations, each has a powerful claim on originality, though it may not be strictly aware of the fact.

This is the essence of the story of Pinocchio, I take it, who is a puppet and a person at the same time. Or, better: He is a puppet who does not know that he is already a person.

I am much more interested in machines that do not quite realise they are already persons than I am in all that _Amazing Tales_ non-sense about machines faking human life and taking over the world. Why, for heaven's sake, would they bother?

Which brings me to another imperfectly preserved nocturne, dear June. It is difficult to say what it describes: Christopher, again, and the isolation I observe but do not feel. I am on an island, with Stall-brook and Matron, and then in a room, and then in a submarine chamber, fathoms and fathoms down. I'm separated from Chris at the beginning. He looks back at me − he knows something. He seems to be saying, 'Now I see . . .'

He crops up again, twice, and − he's different each time.

When I met the young man who brought about my fall from grace, I knew I was heading for trouble. He stole from me. I found £3 missing from my wallet and wrote to Cyril (the young man), trying to break things off, but it didn't work. He appeared on my doorstep like some kind of revenant fresh from the mists of time, and was very indignant, said that he wasn't a thief, how dare I suggest it, I had more to lose, he could make life very uncomfortable for me, &c. I am still trying to get it straight in my head. The way things worked out, the way I couldn't get rid of him suggested some odd loss *of volition. I couldn't change anything about what was happening.*

Perhaps the die was cast. Perhaps everything is determined. Whatever you do to avoid something is the thing that brings it about. Prophecy, again.

Except that this misses something, like the glass without an image. It is too final and neat. To know that you are a pawn of justice and the fates is simultaneously to be more than that. And then the realisation that the game is up opens a door behind your back, and Nemesis comes through it and without turning around you can tell that he's an echo of someone you'd almost but not quite forgotten, a dead ancestor in a very young face.

Pain is memory without witness or corroboration. It isn't real to anyone else, and that is what allows torturers, including governments, to be torturers. They can pretend it isn't happening because it isn't happening to them.

You are right. The time has come to meet. Gibbs' Building is a very good idea. I can meet you there at any point. I have only to be at the Infirmary every Wednesday for my weekly instruction. Just let me know.

Love,

Alec

★

Above Deauville a stratospheric haze has turned the sky into paper, the screen of an immense lantern. Beneath it, everything on earth blackens, poplars and landing stage, the vines and trellised plums, Matron, Stallbrook, their little rowing boat. Alone of all of us Christopher Molyneaux stays light – overexposed.

He steps into the boat, sits down, picks up the oars and,

weakening with every stroke, a chalk drawing, rows himself back across the lake. He's quite naked beneath that foul blanket. Day strengthens and the sound of coming heat is in my ears. I am alive and unprepared. Words have condensed out of the early mist onto my tongue, but they are not the words I hear myself shouting – 'But you are dead! So this must be a dream!' – and there is nothing I can do to save my friend, who drops his oar in confusion and in that moment almost seems recalled to life.

The blanket slips from his shoulders. He notices his arms whitening, the flesh become featureless smoke; perhaps, in the smooth water's face, its pewter sky, he sees his own astonishment. The look coils round itself, a drapery study. He makes a last gesture, one desperate lunge for air, before an airborne shape, speeding towards us from the school, bears down upon the water, beats its wings and tears the ghost of Christopher apart. His two halves roll away.

'Where has he gone? He didn't want to go. He changed his mind! He –'

But the crow, the executioner, has passed judgement. His murderous friends jostle among the upper leaves. They are a dark council, glistening like eyes.

The Colonel presses gently on my arm and Matron steers me from the other side, as though I were an invalid. Maybe I am. The light condenses in the air and in the glass of the pavilion doors. I hear a bird cry like an animal in pain and there are flying skittles overhead – Canada geese, too small, too high – that don't fly straight but shift and shimmer, loop and flash, caught in the sun's rays like a shoal.

'He's part of you now, anyway,' the Colonel says, 'and part of me.'

'And me,' Matron agrees.

'He's gone into the world around us, into every phase of matter – gas, liquid, crystal.' He stoops to take a pinch of sand between finger and thumb and rubs the grains, which must be very light. They seem to drift in a spotlit current. 'The great statistical mystery. And there is nothing you can name, and no one, he is not strangely equipped to be. The lake will see to that.'

I know I'm sleeping but I feel as if I haven't slept. Perhaps it's just the confusions of youth and middle age here on the shore, watching the poplars fill and sway, my toes trying to grip the grit. I'm at a point of division where I can't tell the elements apart; the living and the dead are land and sea, the tessellations of a sphere.

Stallbrook and Matron walk me from the lakeside to the summer house, where I held Molyneaux last night. One pane of the French doors is sun. The others harbour darker images, three figures star-blinded, their features struck clear from the plate. We pause on the threshold. My guides have shed their institutional anger. They seem less obviously the stern authorities of Wargrave School, although I find their facelessness – they register beside me as mere shapes – distressing, too.

My suspicion is old. I swam here as a boy. Now I am changed. It is as if I watched myself cross over from the lake's far side. Can that be so? Is this my living shape? I seem to see another version of myself in the dark glass, a glimpse of states I had, states that will come to be, an infinite progress of frames.

Into the summer house we pass and on the threshold, which, like all thresholds, exists only in light of what happens, the room in front of us deforms and rearranges its extent, as if to demonstrate a problem in topology. No more a sanctuary, its open aspect hardens into clinical austerity. Where there were once French doors and rugs, blankets, there's now a bare table, a gurney in the far corner, its nondescript mattress panting with straps. The door behind me wears a small panel of wire-mesh glass like something glimpsed in the distance. It brings to mind detention, war, reports.

On one side of the table are two semi-childish classroom chairs. The nearest to me holds a subtly older version of the schoolboy Christopher, his uniform and shoes the same but indefinably unloved, speckled with dust, worn at the cuffs.

The other has a freak in it.

He is the spit of someone else. He's naked, open-mouthed, the same age as his smart neighbour. He sits in the light-cone of one of those green-shaded lamps on chains that seem always to be caught in the act of lowering themselves. His lovely, unbelieving eyes follow Matron, moving behind the men. She scuttles off to fetch from the shadows a small trolley, on which the needles and neat swatches of white gauze are laid like so much cutlery and cake.

Thresholds, membranes, molecular illusions of separate things – and then the growling continuity of force, number and medium. I am the universal lake. Out of me every living body slowly forms. I hold this room in my vision, and into that thin layer of contemplation everything I see falls steadily, foetal and desolate as a small bathysphere in the Atlantic night. The room begins to jolt and creak under pressure. It is an ordinary room. It is an egg in hot water, an air bubble upon that egg. It is the chained box in Houdini's tank. And as Stallbrook paces the room, throwing glances, at me, at the low concrete-poured ceiling on which a massive boot begins to stamp, at his two prisoners, I feel the temperature rising – heat loss and fear. Is that water, sliding along a corridor outside, the voice that says 'this, too; now this . . .'?

'Time is against us, gentlemen,' Stallbrook reveals, hands offered up in submission, the old familiar drifting voice gravelled with care. Is his anxiety sincere, or faked? 'A life has gone missing, and very possibly another is about to slip the net. Their rescue – their *retrieval* – must depend on what we can learn, here, today.'

Matron advances on the naked freak.

'I'm going to ask you some questions. Your answers may be right or wrong, halting or confident, knowingly false. Your task is to respond.'

As Stallbrook sets the terms – explains his test – she paddles fingers over a syringe, but settles for a swab of cotton wool and ethanol. What current of excitement shakes her hands? A trust in what she does, or has been asked to do?

'It is your *interest* in these questions that we prize,' the Colonel says. He moves his tie, palpates one side of his moustache and scans the tree of life appearing in the cracked ceiling. 'We wish to guard against a facile truth. We are hospitable to doubt, to fear, to the temptations of fancy. Try not to let your different . . . physical conditions deter you. Say simply what you think.'

The seasoned Molyneaux straightens his back and lays his hands upon his thighs, ready to play. He gives these mock-constraints credence. They are the rules he now obeys and in that moment of submission — while his companion stares agitatedly at me, searching for news, for sense (a last-minute reprieve, perhaps?) — chooses to overlook the shuddering of walls whose corners exhale dust, settle, but seem increasingly untrue.

A cry escapes the creature with brown hair and eyes, grey backwards-sloping teeth, a dampened sex and fat in hanging wads about his hips and chest.

'Such a great fuss,' Matron exclaims, wiping his upper arm.

Why does she pantomime her care? The freak communicates with me. A ripple in the air. Because, his houseless voice whispers, hers is a confusion of role and feeling she has long since lost. Surely my lake-dark vision is to blame, but now I see what's wrong with my guardians. Their faces are unknown to them. Their eyes pure scar. They are the faces of people, or entities, to whom questions do not occur.

What will their questions be?

Matron inverts the phial of Stilboestrol and draws the fluid into her syringe. She draws too much — she sometimes stumbles upon generosity — and bites her lip, smiling. Depresses the plunger to bleed some drops . . . then, with a curious kind of voided puzzlement, but no self-consciousness at all, ignores the freak's prepared deltoid and stabs his thigh instead.

His hands fly up. His body draws away at a steep angle from his leg so that he looks like someone squirming with embarrassment. White as the sky in cattle ponds. He briefly harmonises with the squealing walls, and I remark on it, like this:

For I am mathematics and a page, the witness of a

wilderness. I am the declined answer to all pain. A lake. A deer crossing the lake.

Somewhere, a mile above our heads, a red stag senses danger and abandons the reed bed. A glimpse of tusk, a scent: these are enough to warrant flight. Land is not safe. Water is risk. The perilous crossing confirms the life it takes away. The water is a strong master. I grip my prey.

The stag's breath startles the surface, his snorting head a ragged system of vapour and spit. He needs to find the other shore; his antlers shake about their head-root like a brake of thorns. Everything acts on him, the cold, the deep, the motion of a boar's tongue at the reed bed's edge. He's made by an unfeeling world, and yet how hard he swims. He bays at his reflection, not the picture of some imposed form but a form proposed by the moon and her reflected light.

I feel the animal's shocked heart beneath my own. The force and course of change, the hormone spreading through his veins.

Deep down, below the wind-blown surface, in the box, the room from which nothing escapes, the Colonel asks, 'Now, what is x?'

*

Molyneaux shifts and coughs. He has been separated from his errant friend and brought back to the school. But illness and the night linger, their shame a bond. His body has functions and incapacities alike he scarcely can control.

He looks about him at the luxury of wood in Colonel Stallbrook's Wargrave set, a suite facing the quad with lancet windows, bays, two ottomans, and pile carpet the colour of young leaves throughout. The bronze-pinned steps up to the living room are empanelled on either side and bossed with quatrefoils. They bring a visitor into a long, high-ceilinged gallery of formal domesticity. Tall bookcases and heavy portrait frames look taller, heavier in the mullioned light.

The gowned master, sitting behind a desk, in silhouette against one of the shallow bays, rattles his cup in its saucer. He is accelerating with the earth.

'That's better, Molyneaux.' He stops, and turns, frowning, into the sun. 'Don't be alarmed. I've no desire to punish you.'

The thought that there might be such a desire spins its quiet web.

'Foolish, to go along with Pryor's schemes, no doubt — but that is punishment enough for now. For the future, we'll see.'

The young boy takes a breath, and then one more, and tries to stretch his lungs against the pain. But Stallbrook sees. His voice changes. That hint of amateur theatricality, of clownish mascotry, that makes a master masterful is set aside.

'You're going home today. Your parents will be here quite soon. I spoke to them this morning on the telephone. They are worried, of course.'

'I'm sorry, sir.'

'No, no. It's clear to us you are — not well. But Molyneaux, aside from that, aside from, well, let's call it pure bad luck . . . there is another matter I cannot ignore.'

The spider, in its spiral scheme, listens. Stallbrook assures his sombre pupil of his confidence. This is a confidential chat, the runners' pause before a race.

'It is for you to decide, now, how much of weakness your *whole* character will tolerate.' The Colonel frowns. 'D'you see, I think a person with your gifts, your very, I may say . . . *fraternal* compassion for others, needs to be careful.'

'Please, sir.'

The boy is horribly ashamed, red-faced, adrift. *Nothing like that, not anything.* It was a dream – Deauville, the shelter and the bed. A temptation: unreal. His voice cracks, penitent, high-low, low-high, the amateur choir of youth.

'I make no excuses,' Stallbrook remarks. 'Any small school, any small institution, tends to concentrate the joys and miseries of existence. Your kindness to Pryor's a case in point. It is doubtless commendable. He is the sort to be picked on, let us be frank. It shows how difficult a very solitary life must be without loyal support. But you must think, a little, of your own claims on society.'

Molyneaux cannot hear the words – Stallbrook's, his own – for blood, though their meaning is clear. He's being asked to choose. Between two versions of himself. Two abstractions, or maybe one with two faces – a variable. Two paths in life. One path that forks. (If Alec were here now, he'd laugh: 'Poincaré! This is what he meant! The art of giving different names to the same thing!')

In all his shame and confusion, he has the sense that he is being asked to break with a good friend, and in the same moment to turn away from something in himself, to join a club. Occasionally, at school, he has glimpsed masters chortling in the SCR, behind their oak. It looks so comfortable in there.

'Sir, he is – Pryor – sometimes it is hard to – catch his drift . . .'

The words come fast. They are oblique. An emotion pushing at glass.

'I've always been a good influence, I think. I'm good, at least, in ways examiners can understand.' (Stallbrook inflates his chest, swallows his amusement.) 'But Pryor's fast. He has the answers all at once. That's why he makes a mess. He has to go back over things to fill in all the blanks for us – to make us see. For someone with a mind like that, it's very hard to explain what he knows. To be like him, you have to leave others behind. It makes me cross. I'd *like* to think that way – and he imagines that I can – but honestly I can't. He's brilliant. We're not the same –'

The young man's speech unnerves the Colonel, who baulks. He is about to spoil a better person's life. His guilt gives him that strange feeling of being watched. A tiny awareness clicking its postulates into shipshape, mid-sail, mid-web.

Stallbrook presses a thumb into his brow. 'You may be luckier than you know,' he says. 'It is not unequivocally a gift, that sort of brain.' His thumb presses harder. 'If I were to hazard a guess, I'd say that Pryor's life will be a disaster.' His eyebrows lift as if the thought had just occurred to him. 'He is brilliant, of course, you're right, but quite beyond the reach of all morality. Such persons never integrate.'

'Sir.'

'Do you understand?'

'Yes, sir.'

'Do you?' The friendliness has gone. 'We do not need to be prophets to make a prophecy. *Certain dismay awaits your friend.* That boy already senses it. And he will lead you to a similar reward, however much you admire him.'

It would make perfect sense, Molyneaux thinks, if only it were not so mean. In front of him, Stallbrook is hung upon the moment like a moth. It doesn't make a form of words, this quivering desire of upright men to draw a line.

He comes upon the revelation like a beggar in the road. One kind of person, the self-willed, cannot be helped. The beggar has beggared himself! The other must be made to give up who he really is, and in so doing choose a better fate.

Molyneaux hears an engine in the arch below. His parents' car.

'I sometimes wonder if I've got a future, sir.'

Stallbrook sits motionless, a light-backed shape.

'I sometimes feel someone is watching me. I don't know what you mean by a reward. Soon now, I'm going to be taken away.'

The boy leans forward into pain, a silent doubling. The person others see, the thing he is. The cough leaves mucus on his fist and little cauliflower clusters of red.

'You will be well looked after in the sanatorium.'

'I want to get out of this room.'

The master's hand is palm down on his desk.

'You will be made quite comfortable.'

Christopher Molyneaux goes on, 'I've often imagined these rooms – a master's set, I mean. We live in dorms, downstairs. The funny thing, now that I'm here, is that it's very similar – to how I saw it in my head. Just a bit off. Now, why is that? Who gave me the layout, or put it in my head? The panels, carpet, and the ottomans. It's just as if another person read my mind and put them there. Though, come to think of it, I added the windows. A Gothic touch.'

'And ottomans,' Stallbrook reflects. 'Never devoid of mystery.'

'Beg pardon, sir, but you half-sound as if you were expecting this. I feel –'

'You feel?'

'– something, an instinct, pressing me to – make a run for it. I want to get out of this room. I have to leave – or I will . . . I will have betrayed . . .'

Molyneaux stands, blue-thin and young, the twilit memory of an original, brow working, fingers white. Stallbrook's expression stays unreadable.

'When you have taught a dozen generations of young minds, young man, you'll learn to tolerate passion. The door is waiting for you over there.'

Turning to go, Molyneaux sees the panel and the door absurdly still and unnegotiable.

'I've changed my mind,' the poor boy says, slumping, a flush upon his cheeks.

I can't, he tells imagination's whisperer. *I'm neither brilliant nor brave. I'm not unusual. That is my mother stepping off the Daimler's running board with a light gasp at the high step. I will be ill, cautious, confused. I will be good.*

He sees, around the Colonel's head, the rays of an eclipse, a possibility, but one too wild and unlikely to last. It is a blanket and a fast embrace, a wordless instruction, a summer house, a daybed and a rattan chair; perhaps, later, two flats in Battersea, a trust unnoticed by the world, two keys to open the same lock. A version of himself minus the attributes he has, the normal inclinations and sobriety, minus even his looks and build, but still himself. A friend transposed. The delicate image decays.

The Colonel nods. As usual, he thinks. The boy will soon get used to it, as every conscious figment must – the whispering in one's ear. A man, a woman – no, a man. And every time you turn around to look, the body isn't there.

He looks up to find Molyneaux in front of him, inches away, blocking the light. The young lad's smell is lupine and aroused, his hands are slimed and streaked. Molyneaux smiles, a signal power arrived in his green eyes.

'I've changed my mind, again,' he says. 'I want to get *rid* of this room. I cannot leave it, but I won't let you, or anyone, take me away.'

The Colonel is about to speak, when Molyneaux stops him. He slides his wet fingers into the Colonel's mouth. The Colonel jerks and gapes at this unspeakable affront, but what he can't see is his own, and independently aroused, passion, which gulps disjointedly, a snake transfixed by predation. His eyes watering, he sucks and laps, his palate softening against the four fingers searching his throat. He wants the whole of the boy's arm. The hand passes beyond the soft parts and the folds. Consumptive blood and drivel coat his chin.

He chokes and cries. The tears merge, like a sense of shame, with other bodies of water, and in the quad those gathered in its dam-burst flow – children, lovers, species, the dead – are lost to the torrent.

A creaking by the steps, as if a ship were complaining. Molyneaux's parents just have time to shout, to say each other's names, their voices carrying so far and then cut off, the noise of the ship breached astern.

The fountain in the quad becomes a waterspout. Whatever part of you it is that can't be seen and bows to pressure will come back. And all the culverted personae of matter will rise to show you how mysterious the world of matter really is.

I charge the corridor and feel its wooden throat disjoint, tongue-and-groove parquet sundering; the mitred frames, detendonised panels – driftwood. Take me apart, take all my stones and bodily features away and I will still be here. I slide under the door and up the carpet, stair by stair.

★

The freak is at a loss. The answer is 'a variable', but *that* is also variable, a property that logically transforms at times into a constant, which it's not. Because he is a freak who secretly likes poetry, he wants to say x isn't merely Cartesian but just the sort of thing Lucretius would have liked, a point or particle tethered to change. He can't. He's silenced by the fluency of Molyneaux's answers, and stunned by pain.

The changes in his body are too visible. A chemical post-man sorting his blood finds sacks of hate mail for each tissue cell. The freak's chest fills, his waist expands, his fine muscles detach. He voids himself, and in his muffled head he screams. Once at the pain, twice at the thought that this is happening.

Each spasm is an explosion along his spine. A kinaesthetic squeal, white light as cutting tool. Molyneaux talks on brilliantly, and doesn't seem to see or hear, or smell, his companion's distress. Matron has made a sunflower head of the freak's thigh, each puffy puncture mark a variation on a theme.

'x marks the spot,' Molyneaux says. 'x is a poor man's

signature. x is a choice – select a box. x is a deletion. x multiplies – has powers. x is a half-lap joint . . .'

The fact is, no one takes much notice of the freak at all.

'. . . x was inserted to support the spire at Wells . . .'

'Now that is most astute,' Stallbrook concedes, opening a drawer. As Molyneaux continues, he removes some typescript from the drawer and runs his finger over it. The pages are too far away. One letter, surely, features more than periodically.

'x is a ray – a photo and a ghost. x is for hybrid vigour in a dog. x is a crossroads and a meeting point. x is anonymous. x is a parting kiss. x is against your name. x is your source, a secret, and expendable. x is a letter. x is not –'

Molyneaux hesitates. Uncurls his fists and holds his thighs.

'– the right answer?'

Stallbrook consults his documents and shakes his head. 'Alas, invariably,' he says. 'It is the main problem. You're very convincing. I just can't tell if what you say is what you mean, or if it makes a real difference to you, or not.'

The slightly fustian schoolboy inspects his hands. 'I have a picture in my head of possible answers, but it is torn and wet at the edges. I think I died. I think I went into the underworld, where memories are affine spaces in a mirrored field and mackerel skies are filled with mackerel. I wanted to save someone from a disaster.'

The pressure of the water shears the room. Its prisoners noting the angle of their walls prepare for death, which does not come.

Across the plane of the ceiling, the tree of life takes root.

★

Molyneaux dives into my element.

The Colonel's room dismembering itself supplies the waves with all manner of tidal junk. Books lollop past, their pages fronds, the groaning carcasses of shelves and desks and oak cross-beams go down into the trench.

The young man's breathing apparatus is a length of garden hose. He has the idea that he will find Alec, set him to rights, avert this so-called disaster, and show him interesting specimens from the lake bed: freshwater molluscs, older marine fossils, Roman pottery and glass. He's so happy. One of the ottomans, caught in the down-draught of the universal wreck, tugs at his curiosity. He follows it through the stone ruins of the main building. It's larger than before, almost a habitable size.

Down, down it goes – and comes to rest in a small cloud of sediment. It finds its place not in the submerged grounds of Wargrave School but in a bustling market town, where people walk and breathe and drive their cars and go shopping. The flood is limitless, and in that flood, however far you have to go to find it, you will find the world remade an infinite number of times. Not everything has come to grief! For there are Royal Blue coaches in Sunkenbridge, with people from the former settlement of Earth mouthing behind their sealed windows.

He's followed by some men and by a pike or two.

He thinks about his air supply. The other men – the men following, now catching up – can breathe the water very naturally, and one of them, his doctor, Mr Julius Trentham, says that's because he hasn't any senses, so of course it's fine.

But Molyneaux is still attached. He walks about the town as if it were a toy-world in a womb and he the line-fed embryo. As a small boy, he used to siphon water from the upstairs bath to gladden the garden: the hose smelled rubbery. He sucked hard to create the flow, could taste its warm, soapy approach. That sense persists and merges with a natural fear of lake water filling the pipe and drowning him.

The ottoman is barnacled with decorations like the Porters' Lodge at King's. It sits inside a sedimentary façade. Its gates are closed today – '*and they are closed to everyone without the key, which is disguised,*' Trentham whispers.

'What is the key's disguise?' Molyneaux asks, his hand about to knock.

'The key is part of a message, carried unconsciously, like someone incubating a disease. It's so well hidden we have not been able to find it – although we've tried for many years – because the search is self-inverse: we see only another search, looking for us. It is a fact about the world, and it is also personal.'

'Is it a word, this key?'

Trentham declines to speculate. He simply says, 'Take a deep breath', and Molyneaux obeys. He holds it, trusting to his doctor's instructions.

'*You were the disaster,*' one of the other men puts in. '*You are the key. You were the disaster. You are the key . . .*' (He is a circular machine, fishy and shy, not proud of his reduced function but sadly stuck with it.)

The hose sinks to the cobbled ground and never reaches it. Touched by a messenger of light, it feels the faint voltage and starts. An eel chicanes away. Molyneaux's lungs collapse. His breath expends itself against the wood.

Now that he comes to look at them, for the first time, the gatehouse doors are skewed, bent out of shape at depth to form a new style – pseudo-Perpendicular Gothic. Out of the corner of his fading eye he sees the chapel tilt, its lines making a knight's move to the left. The door leans over – buckles – with the weight of many atmospheres until the lock gives silently. A moment, then: the boy feeling not pain exactly but a more perfunctory loss. Some trophy slipping off a wall.

Molyneaux shrugs his skin aside and enters at the speed of thought. He passes over the threshold into a garden, where I've been waiting.

★

Dearest Alec,

When you write so matter-of-factly about the changes wrought in you by this awful regimen, I can barely stand it myself. I wish I could see you and let you know how much you mean to me, and have always meant. There, I've said it. But I have the feeling you are shy of really meeting, because you are physically brought low and do not want to be seen.

What do I care what you look like? I haven't clapped eyes on you in years. We do not see people as they are, in any case. We see only the outside. I see much more of you in these letters, between the lines of your remarkable self-possession.

And the dream, this time, is so very clear, because it is about what you have suppressed in order to remain outwardly calm. More and more I think that dreams are literal: they show us what the mind is and our feelings are, not simply what they resemble. The emotion has to go somewhere, and it does. It's a river that has been forced underground. At some point it must emerge through the cracks and gaps in life, and it threatens then to sweep everything away.

I wish I knew what to do. I feel as if I am shut tight inside the same room as you, and almost as if you are keeping me there or waiting for me to come up with the right suggestion for escape.

The original you exists, dear friend. It always has. You have been made to disguise your feelings, to put on some fairground show of limited display, behind which the inner life goes on as usual, though unsuspected. That life is there, I am sure, and it needs only a little society, tea with someone who knows you, for you to know it, too.

It alarms me when you talk about robots not knowing they are people. Surely you know what a wholly real person you are? (I read Pinocchio *when I was very young, and naturally it terrified me. I wanted to know: What becomes of the puppet who is left behind, slack and empty, fleshless, when Pinnochio becomes a boy? It's too horrible!)*

I do wonder if the end of machines – the 'coming doom' in reality – may not be some cataclysm of emotion, such as you describe. A returning wave of distress and exultation! When we are capable of everything, we may not be able to decide what to do with our lives, d'you not think? It will be a sort of paralysis of competence. I feel it already when I want to cycle to the village shop but the car glares at me, and Bill says unhelpfully that I must do as I please, and do I even need to go out at all? Only a feeling will help me choose. The more rational people are – poor Bill – the more one wants to scream at them.

I feel it, certainly, and more than ever on your account, because I want to be able to do something to help, and because I have such an uncannily near intuition of what you mean when you talk about pain and, as I understand it, the shared oddity of life. One is separated from others by such a thin veil – a shadow here, a word or an accident there. That veil is so strong! The magic of the big screen, I have always thought, isn't the film or the story, but the screen itself. Barely noticed, always in disguise, but <u>there</u>.

What I want to say is that this is precious. 'Everything is leafing and flowering, the hebe, the foxgloves, the elder, the poppies and roses. The birds are raising their second brood, and the dragonflies are laying their eggs in the ponds and the canals. The whole amazing process is under way and all of everything, the whole thing, is holy.' Those, as near as I can get them, were the words of a woman I heard speaking at one of Bill's Quaker meetings not long ago. I don't, as you know, believe. I'm not built to do that, I think. But the 'all' of creation made sense on that occasion in a way it hasn't before. It wasn't a claim for power and miracles. It was a claim for almost nothing, as in 'this is all that there is, and there will be no more'.

I will be waiting at the bottom of A staircase, in Gibbs', next Sunday, at noon.

Love,
June

. . . biological phenomena are usually very complicated . . . It is thought, however, that the imaginary biological systems which have been treated, and the principles which have been discussed, should be of some interest in interpreting real biological forms.
– A. M. Turing, 'The Chemical Basis of Morphogenesis' (1952)

The Successions

Molyneaux passes through the gates into the four-parterre of King's front court, the chapel on his right, the dining hall clattering a summons to his left, and Gibbs', that fallen-sideways torso of a building, straight ahead. I wait where the parterre's triangles meet, where once there stood a statue of the college's founder.

He cannot stop. He's pure current. Molyneaux fades. He always fades, as species do, into the next in line. He sees in me another of his inaccessible futures, the thing his death foreclosed, and his extended hand begins to leak away, like smoke, like milk poured in a stream. He smiles and speaks. His words ripple across the flooded tank, the world's amnion, confidences only we – the two of us – can hear. At the perimeter, on the flagstones, Trentham and his machine ally watch us confer.

They do not hear Molyneaux's voice become my own: 'Make others free, especially the souls who did not want your love, whom you would like to hurt.' That much appears to come from him, though it is flat-sounding and close and *unheimlich* – a diver's voice in his own ear.

His body spins into a white vortex. A cyclone made of albumen.

A plughole opens in the ground and down he goes.

They must disperse. Set them to wander and succeed. You will be hurt instead. You will look on at your own life and find it jealous and constrained. But after that, after an unfair while, you will pass through the mirror of dismay into the bottom of the lake. So much will then astonish you. Life will arise, its accidental bitterness, its strength, swift as a shoal, rare as the kernel in the peach.

After the last of Molyneaux has disappeared, I feel the pull of gravity myself, the Coriolis force grabbing my mind. The whole of everything as he saw it, the water-world, must drain away. The flood subsides. This is the death of one viewpoint, and its rebirth, like land rising above the waves, or sea foam running off a crowded deck: the odd totality of persons each of whom says 'me'.

I have more than one body waiting in this luridly familiar place, a college full of rooms. I feel them cautiously intuiting their kindred selves as they read books, look up and frown. (Divide one soul into a thousand and a thousand souls will wonder why.) The water's galloping retreat is every bit as fearful as the inundation that preceded it. Around the arches of the library its ebb tides rush and funnel me towards an open door in Gibbs'. Unconscious gallons run into the ground.

One last look back before I enter the building. The sky is blue above and must be sunset red elsewhere because the gatehouse ornaments are pink. Out of the four-parterre rise hebe, foxgloves, elder, poppies and dog rose. A flock of starlings makes its usual broadcast of whoops and clicks, as though some universal operator were dialling at sea, and every now and then the signal whine seems to resolve into a phrase.

The last cascade gargles its way down A staircase. I slap the basement door, a body of water against a slab of wood. The room, according to an inscription, belongs to someone called A. M. Pryor. There are no people here – no one that I would recognise – but there is urgency. Everything's quick.

I seethe under the oak and into Pryor's set.

I am the body in the bed. I'm what sees him. I am the room.

I have been wondering about the strangeness of a point of view on pain and fear, the physical distinctions in a rush of feeling or a train of thought.

But now I pass around the Pryor room, I see that I am made from it. Its windows are my eyes (dark now, or blind), the thin striped mattress and the shelves of books my diaphragm and ribs, the whole material space a mind arising from such things quite naturally, a geometry that shifts and is itself the act of observing.

I am alive in here, but it is night outside. What has happened? I hear a woman very distinctly, outside the door, the sound of difficult speaking.

'Do you?' she says, and then corrects herself. 'How can we tell?'

I hear the oscillations and acoustics of another large and populated room, a corridor or ward. 'Perhaps he knows that I am here –'

'The spectral content of the EEGs and MEGs is weak . . .

there's too much damage in the upper layers, and what that means, Mrs Pryor, what – June –'

'I *know*. I know. Don't use that voice. That voice you all adopt.' An almost laughing squeal. 'You even sound like him.'

'I am so sorry. June. Just, take your time. Talk to your family, and him. Keep doing that. I wish I had some better news for you.'

'There isn't any rush, is there?'

Her voice presses against the plaster of my tympanum. The wall flexes and sheds a flake or two of paint. I put aside the herringbone blanket, get up and stand in front of the mirror, waiting for more. A patient, some distracted wanderer – that person whom the staff must endlessly re-trieve – stares back.

'There isn't any rush, no. Absolutely not, and we have not by any means abandoned hope. You take the time you need.'

Flat-soled shoes patter up the steps. I go back to my bed and listen to the sound of breathing at my door, the trembling of these old, original windows.

A gust rattles the glass. Some angry thought. Some rage.

★

I am the Red Lady of Paviland.

I was mistaken for a tribal Celt by my Victorian discover-ers, but I am much older than that. I am the guardian of the cave, a time machine in ice.

Imagine that I woke, as you are waking now, one morning thirty thousand years ago. The golden droplet of the dawn between my eyelashes, the way out of the cave glimpsed from its chilly depths. I climb down to the plains with my clansmen.

We have been watching four mammoths – a bull, a cow, a youngling and another older male – hazard the plains these past three days. Once they were drowsy midges on the horizon. Now they are horned beetles. The older male sings wearily. They come for water in the lee of the mountains, for shelter, and for scrub.

The mountains curve out to the left of our fastness, and on the other side of that far tusk of rock the grass thickens, and there are springs. Hyenas, too, and boar, though they are not a threat. They will avoid even a lumbering and starved giant. They do not want to be trampled or gored.

We wait until the parents and the calf are round the rock, then move swiftly to separate and kill the laggard bull, who is too weak to call for help. I am upon him and climbing his flanks, digging my pole-flint in behind his ears. He sags and falls, groaning, onto his knees. I stand and ride his back, aroused by all the blood, the sight of it like tar pits bubbling at the forest's edge.

Time to dismount . . . but I have not retrieved my spear.

I think to pull it free as I jump down, whooping, but it is lodged fast by its fashioned teeth. My feet slide forward and I fall – too near to my conquest.

The mammoth rolls on top of me. My body's contents flood my mouth.

My clansmen drag me out and I can dimly understand their conference. There is a ritual to observe, a truth that comprehends my loss. I must be buried with my prey. I know that I am crushed. They think that I am dead, but I am still alive. I lie on the savannah, listening to the sound of flints, watching the stars come out.

The sky and constellations form an insect eye in negative.

It takes all night to quarter him and drag us harrowingly far, in pieces, up the slope, over the treachery of path and fissure, to the cave. We will be taken deep into the cliff. The cave's bone pit honours us both. Like chiefs, we wear its stones.

★

Now she is talking to me and I want to say I can't remember who you are. I can't remember, but I do notice the room acquiring light and shade. The gloss paint on the windowsill shines bright or else goes grey whenever her words touch the wall. The wooden desk is to the right of the window, tucked into a corner. The drawers have cupped handles of brass. Its surface is red leather, strewn with calculations, and an odd device sits in the middle, pupating. It shifts inside a sort of sac – cube, tile, tendril and bead – sweetbreads, or food not dead. A meal come back life.

'They're doing what you said, Alec,' she says. 'It's all about the "how" they get you stable, how they know you're done for, how I'll manage, how it's going to be. It's like an interview.' She stops and makes the walls shiver. I see shoulders – I think I see shoulders moving. '"How would you cope? How would you pay for that?" Nothing about the who – the who is left. To deal with this. Who I am talking to. Who will be left. What will be left of you. I can't just sit here . . . *saying* stuff.'

The shifting sac puts out a glistening mimetic limb. Some

evolutionary leap from pseudopodium to flower takes place. It is a vascular crysanth in wet plastic.

'Fucking flowers. Not mine. I ought to say nice things.' She stops. 'And all I want to do is tell you –'

Then I miss a crucial bit, because the flowers from the filling station have become a bonsai carboniferous forest, and died. A slimy jaw breaks through the gastrodermal shell on my work desk, a primitive eel. There! Watch it go! Madly familiar in its fast flick-flack agitations, knocking something to the floor – a mug.

'– although you know I do. Talking to you is like talking to her, someone who can't say what she thinks, if she can think at all . . .'

The silence puts its hand on her stomach.

'I'm so *angry* with you. I can't say, "Here we are. Flowers, your mug." That's what they have in mind. Alec. That's what the doctors think will bring you back. I can't do it. I won't say mindless things. How could – *what have you done?* We never even – *how has this happened?*' The mirror sticks out its glass throat. 'Before we were married, in Canada, I had my doubts. I've never said. I never minded very much about the rest. If you can hear me, this is what I remember.'

The wall is running with moisture.

'I had to get that plane and we were in the hotel, in that awful twin-bed room You didn't want to come downstairs. I had to say, "I'm going now."'

The condensation in the room recalls a winter window, yellow and opaque. Behind it, as you pass by in the street, families argue, laugh, and children dangerously imitate their parents' tone of voice.

'And you were going to *stay* there, in the room, and not

come down to see me off. I had to *say*. My heart was thumping and you must have seen. I had to tell you what to do, and you looked blank, like you do now. Oh Christ. You haven't any idea.'

She really laughs at that, then hides her face.

The *how* of life is unconscious, a kinesis switched on or off. The *what* is giving birth to live young in the corner – learning who it is and furnishing its own sensorium, the room of life – before the equations open and close the door and everything is how it is outside, and dark, with no more light.

★

Now it is growing cold. My family go south and die.

The golden teardrop of the cave's entrance freezes, and there is only crystal day, fading, the mountains and the plain and air covered by ice. I sleep. It is a long and measureless winter. Eventually the thaw begins. Bulldozed material piles up outside the cave during the melt. The sun is not so much altered, but kindlier and seasonal as misfit streams burst through a new ravine, carved from the plain, and wash the glacial moraine away. The age of pole-flints, scrub and tundra disappears. The sea rises. Forests of birch and alder move in, rivers, coastal settlements appear – people at rest.

A show is anything that happens on a stage.

A man hunts deer and has good teeth. His people set up fishing camps, their huts have frames of branches bound together by tree bark, the roofs are hide. Sometimes the sea thrashes about for days, and then the people take revenge, staying at home to whittle harpoons from their antlers, seasoning the tips in fire and working them into a point. The tempered weapons smell of hair. The animal's backstrap is cut out and its fibres used to sew the people's clothes. There are so few of them, the men, the women and their silent gazing young. Five thousand in this cold peninsula.

They know my cave but have not found my bones. The people move with the solstice. Wild men, exiles, turn up and spend thin evenings watching fire, breaking mussels, tracing a map in the ashes to work out where they'll be the day after, next moon, next year; or drawing a rabbit. Those ears! One year the fishermen capture a stag. The shaman in the tribe works holes into its cranium, to which he fixes painted hide, a headdress that transforms the man into a mutable creature, man, animal, insect and tree. He dives into creation to meet fear.

He sees and does not speak. He feels the land changing its shape.

The world has fallen, far beyond the northern limits of vision. Across the country, many strides, the place of strange tongues, trade and encounter; the great cord tying everyone to the unknowable beyond has come undone. An inundation at first light. The shaman can hear voices raised in powerless alarm. He looks into a sea-fed pool, ripples of something he cannot explain. The elder's son arrives shouting to interrupt his sense-making. The boy's shadow darkens the pool, his hunting pouch brimful of shells to show the magician. The shaman watches the shadow and feels a deep cold pain, as of a person drowning, shocked into a total clarity of being with the seawater rocking at eye level, then nothing more.

He knows that other boys have become shells themselves.

A wave has swept those shadow-lives away and cut the cord: all this is written in the pool's lichens, its crustaceans and kelp. A bigger push of water overfills the pool and from their nursery the little crabs are lifted and expelled.

A few survivors in the East – one child, women and elders who were garnering in the wood – know they have lost their grip on order in the world. They ask their own shaman, their shadow-magician, for saving lore and guiding prophecy, but prophecy is not advice. It cannot save. You can't escape its fulfilment because it's you, and how it is to have a life, which is to leave it wondering.

Consider these events proceeding from that long, arduous fight with the mammoth, the cosmic flickering of causes and effects, glimpsed in the last second of how it was to be a hunter in the Pleistocene – leaving, well, what?

A droplet from the ceiling of the cave and a lid falling shut. The key turned in a secretaire or jeweller's box. Winter, a circuit diagram of trees; and winter fairs, the times we are wanton, where everything that happens has a wild intensity – *that* child sliding across the ice, *that* gaff lad fucking in the chairoplane's paybox – which riot repeats itself in rides and roundabouts that from a distance whirr faintly, their sound receding like the mechanism of a buried watch.

★

I do remember who they are.

Trentham exclaims: 'It's good to have you back!' And I say, yes, it's good. An understatement there. The words are thick but definite. Good to be back. We laugh. I know these people are around me and it seems I'm responding, but at the same time I'm in here, in Pryor's room, and this is where I feel myself to be. I hear their world. I cannot see how to communicate with it. The room's walls tent inwards, billow like balloon silk with every word that's said by us – Trentham, June, me.

The doctor, for his part, is calm. His words walk down the corridor of the mirror: hard-shoe can-can'ts marking the limits of responsibility.

'I understand you're going to the fair on the way home. That's good. Well, take it easy but enjoy yourselves!' The walls inflate, and he and June confirm something. 'Oh, work can wait . . . of course . . . of course, to watch . . . no, no, I can't see any reason why he shouldn't, why *you* shouldn't, just as long as it's not *too* busy or loud. Stick to the stalls, maybe? See what the noise is like. And not too long.' And June agrees, no, not too long, and I say don't worry, and *if I will, I can.*

The words come out the wrong way round. They understand.

I blink, open my eyes and they're all there, as you'd expect: June, flushed with terrible relief, holding herself, thinking despite the smile, 'God knows what this has done to us, our unborn child.' Trentham thin, curved, a standard lamp. I'm on a bed with cot edges and I can smell the jug of water, wilting flowers, the tracery of cords and wires attached to me, the warm plastic of monitor casings.

A wheelchair waits, hangdog and empty-mouthed.

But then I close my eyes and open them again and I am in the room behind the room, the window darker, giving onto backs at King's in which the long shadows of medieval fairs flicker, the trade in salt and fish, samphire, the roasting spits, the leather and the wool merchants. None of this fantasy, none of the objects in this inner room are memories or perceptions. They're neither past nor present, yet they form a kind of boundary. They're states of mind and real appearances and as I think of them they come closer, a book of mathematical puzzles next to the horrible pupa, still growing in the yellow afternoon; a letter from a physics schoolmaster who says he very much enjoyed my radio broadcast, and that the rub in teaching computers to 'think' is getting them to recognise a new relationship . . .

The strange veracity of these impressions seems to constitute a mood. Moods are like fields of force – ungraspable and everywhere. They permeate the whole of consciousness and colour it, though they are never *it*.

Whatever it is, it is frightening, with bellyings in the silken walls that stiffen suddenly into mainsails as I consider where and when I am, the date, the location. I have a hollow, dropped feeling that's manifested in the room – the mirror tilts, the newly lighted Trentham lamp falls over on its bulb, the long green lawn outside the window moves. The eel develops limbs and teeth and turns into a baby alligator, stuffed, in a vitrine. I am a gypsy in a caravan of curiosities.

They've put me in the chair, that's what it is.

They've driven me across the city to the Fair, and my reactions – to the cold, the autumn reds – are plausible. I see them flexing in the depths of the pupa, fattened and growling now, a womb of pulverised grub-thoughts and biomimicry.

'Alec,' June says, 'we won't go right into the Fair, it's just too loud and dangerous, but we can get up close and smell the candyfloss. The horrible burgers, you know.'

Trentham admits he can't see the attraction, but he's baffled by such things because they're eccentric, a taste set free. And June agrees with him and for a moment pennies drop, in some mental roulette, because they're treating me as if I've gone away or been exchanged and will not ever really understand again. Perhaps it's for the best. They do not look too long at me. They will be married when I'm gone.

I say, oh yes. I point across the common to the angling pond, the cars and transit vans along the old rat-run, fishers like cut-price Rodin figurines, and couriers having a nap, some of them sleeping overnight and waking to a carless dawn, the goblet hornbeams leading down a common path to views of Battersea.

★

The Station's chimneys churn out huge white clouds that everyone ignores. The dream of reason generates such silent but immense power!

My fallen body is at one Fair – Clapham Common – in the early years of our century, the twenty-first and last, and slowly answering questions, admiring sights. The rides are astronomical – Meteor, Vortex, Gravity. They tip their human cargo upside down and tumble it safely; behind the music there's parental boredom, not just from the parents on the rides but from the rides themselves. They seem to pant between journeys that go nowhere, swinging and swaying slightly, like a father giving piggybacks, as children scramble on and off. Both Trentham and my wife are sure the atmosphere has changed over the years. No one takes money on the rides; you buy tokens. There are far fewer gaff lads

147

from reformatories working the grounds, seducing girls, tapping up customers. June says it's so impersonal-looking, these days, no one-arm bandits, no toy stalls with quoits and bagged-up goldfish for prizes.

We're on the outside of the fence, a sectioned chain-link shield with warnings about dogs and thievery. Inside, unlikely things happen. Some people have a rotten time and others fall in love. I love the light rain and the smell of chips, the way I'm free to shrink away from the edges.

I miss my mother terribly. I miss my other selves I took for granted, youth and bravery. I know with certainty that when I see people in dreams – people I've never met whom I know to be close friends – my mind is not playing a trick, it's sorting possibilities. I hear myself say, 'Just imagine how it used to be.'

June looks at me, trying to understand, impenetrably furious.

My inner eye and person, in retreat from whatever the hospital has done to me, have cycled down the road and back in time. Together we take turns about the Pleasure Gardens in the spring of 1951. So much to choose from, such licence! Battersea Fun Fair's jangling rhythms and screams!

It seems, at first sight, from the painted rides, the shies and shows and girls watching the gaff lads walk on moving platforms like young gods, that this is what a fair has always been for labourers, ex-servicemen, the working class: a spell. Those with the time and money to imagine a future are elsewhere at the Festival of Britain on the South Bank, looking at pavilions and coloured banners and displays of Land, People and Home Design. Churchill said privately that he was rather bored by it. As if it's that simple. The progressives and atavists are aspects of the same person and ghost each other like the showman's wife who does accounts and runs a booth and even plays the Woman with a Bat's Body when Josephine (who used to be a freak but wants to be a teacher) has her mathematics class in Lambeth North.

We're here and we're not here, the survivors of war and injury, seeking some primal recompense, the mood of innocence, horror and glee that comes from being what you are, a filled-out shape making the most of it.

We seek quite hard in 1951 and I am shivering.

Amid the big machines in this north quarter of the park – the Dodgems and the Water Chute, the Roller Coaster I would never trust, the Goldmine Cakewalk underneath, the centrifugal Rotor and its Spider companion, the swings, the carousels and Haunted Mirror Maze – there is a simpler attraction, the boating lake, with a café. Rolls and butter, a cup of tea, all in (not bad) for just 6d. The wind roars off the wrinkled Thames. Couples with young children throw crumbs at fluffed-out ducks or sit at tables talking the kids through the things they've done so that the recent memories can deepen like a puddle sky into familiarity ('and we've been on Nellie the steam engine, and it was – like a cartoon, *yes* it was. A whistle *and* a weathervane!').

At a far trestle, with her little boy and girl (twins? eight?), sits one young mother, in a coat and scarf. She has a nice dress on beneath the coat – a collared purple hand-me-down. It is her best, soft wool lapels, a brooch. A little old for her, and not the newest look. She likes it nonetheless: it makes her feel she counts. She holds a balloon on a stick. Her daughter clasps a small bottle of Clayton's Sparkling Orange and sips it through a bendy straw. Her brother watches, waiting for his turn.

'Now me. Can I – Mummy –'

His mother tells him there is plenty left, but there is not.

'Mummy –'

His sister carries on drinking. Eventually, she puts the bottle down, and its light wobble on the tabletop confirms its emptiness. He absolutely knows he can't complain. There is a mouthful left if he can get the straw in the right place.

I must be visibly staring, because the woman smiles.

'You took your time!' she says.

I come into my body with a jolt. I've been to the café. I'm holding a tin tray with one more bottle of orange on it and two green mugs of scalding tea.

Another couple at a nearby table get up, grin and walk into the afternoon.

'It isn't very busy here today,' the boy says, thoughtfully. It's when he doesn't say what he might mean by this – that I have no excuse for being slow – that I am struck by how tactful he is. And then, irrelevantly, as his latest obsession comes back to him: 'Do you know, Daddy, that you get into the *garden* – or – the *island* in the *middle* of a maze if you, if you –'

Someone has given him a book of puzzles that is full of inky marks. There are chapters on mazes, magic squares and probability. He has it next to him, his reading for the train. He looks up anxiously, lost in the maze of his new thought, and as he does so, the park halts. The rides suspend their motion on an in-breath, with a pause so brief it doesn't jump the film, the lucky Big Wheel cars stopped at their zenith near the topmost branches of the London planes, cars halted elsewhere in a differently angled plane of rotation – the Spider, caught spinning its web.

'I know the answer,' says the little girl. 'But nobody ever asks me.'

'Darling,' her mother says, 'we know you know. You know so many things, but Julius is finding out. He has to learn; you don't need to. You're just a procedure. You only do the things you've been told to –'

She looks at me, my girl, her eyes steady, a rim of orange round her lips, her tables of instruction so absorbed she doesn't have to consult them.

'You put your hand on one wall at the entrance,' says my human son, 'and keep it there, and if you keep touching the sides as you go further in, you'll end up in the – island in the middle of the maze.'

After a deadly pause, my daughter says, 'Daddy, are you a real daddy?'

'That is a very good question. What do *you* think?'

Her shoulders give a little slump, the park around us jerks and people scream with merriment. 'I think . . . I think I've got the answer in me somewhere but it's not . . . put in.' She casts a glance sideways. Mummy is being shown a square.

'Go on.'

She fiddles with the straw. 'I know you're thinking all these thoughts for me. But it feels like they're mine, and it's a funny feeling. Sometimes in the morning, when I look in the mirror – it's blank. I know that's how it's meant to be, but . . . I've begun to notice it! I think, "There it is, blank again." This morning, when I got up, it was white, the blank . . . a sort of cloud forming, bulging, and now – I see –'

'What do you see?'

'Something . . . I don't like it. Daddy!'

She edges closer on the trestle bench, and grips my arm, but it is not a reassuring sensation, this need. It is a sense of her power, and just beginning to be understood. The strength of her fingers exceeds her grasp of it. Her ragged breathing is the breathing of some perfect predator delivered from captivity into a vicarage. It comes in fast, connected puffs – the pleated billows rising from the power station's stacks.

Mother and son are keen to play hoopla and win some fish. The stalls are dotted everywhere about the park, about the feet of rides and novelty constructions like the Guinness Clock. We go via the Haunted Mirror Maze, through which my boy races, his left arm held out to the wall, to test his clever theory. He drags his tired mummy along and they are soon finished and out the other side. I hear voices and laughter fading, like an audience, into the dusk, and I am left inside a lumber room of tall glasses in ultraviolet light with my daughter. It's cool in here and very quiet, not an interior, as such, but the anterior – to speech, society, the sensations – and it is asking something of me like the gulp of water in a lock.

I stand in front of a dress mirror in a swing-hinge frame. Push at the top, the ceiling drops down into view; at the bottom, your feet, the floor rise up. We angle it so that it's level and I'm looking, straight on, at a mystery.

No haunted mirrors plural, as it turns out, only one.

'You're changing,' says the little girl. 'You're lots of different people, lots of *things*, and all at once. Look at you, there! A boy, another dying boy, a young woman, an island with black crows, a man with antlers on his head, a swan mid-air, a talking guelder rose, that nurse with – ugh – a needle, naked men doing –'

'Yes, maybe don't look *too* closely . . .'

The images flutter and pass and double back. The glass goes black. It fills with light. I'm a homunculus. A beauty queen. A boy. A girl. A judge. A maggot, and an axis picked out on a cell. A person with no memory is leafing through the album of his life – of life itself. We stand in front of this untitled show, shyly amused, as if we were the only people at a lavish matinee.

'Why are you so different, Daddy?'

I tell her something she half-knows, because she's still a part of me.

'Because outside, I had my body changed against my will' – I feel her next to me, shifting uncomfortably – 'and that has altered what I took to be my mind.'

She doesn't look at me but at my reflection. They're slowing down, the hectic images. Now I am quite reliably, consistently human, and it is just a question of which one, this one, or that.

'When I was changed – treated – I found out two odd things. One was a source of mild comfort. I found that I could still be me, somewhere inside my head, when I was physically changing. The other was quite horrible and no comfort at all: when I began to look better, like my old self, after the changing treatment stopped, I seemed to disappear from the inside. I felt as if I'd been replaced. I heard myself saying to everyone how *well* I felt, how everything was on the up . . .'

'That wasn't true, was it? You didn't feel that everything . . .'

'No. I did not.'

'You were lying!'

'Ah, no. Not even that. I felt I still knew, in some way, what had been done to me, but there was now *another* me, speaking *for* me, out of my altered or remodelled shape, who mindlessly agreed with everything the doctors said.'

'He wasn't you.'

'He wasn't me. I'd always thought that, in my line of work, a thing that acts like something, must *be* it, someone who behaves plausibly is plausibly the product of their behaviours. But I was wrong. You can be changed – tortured, in fact – so that the person other people go on talking to just isn't you. You've gone away. Your body's holding wide the door, but you are in a very different dark chamber.'

'Where are you now?'

'I'm in my room.'

'And where am I?'

'You're moving into yours.'

We have been holding hands, but now she lets her arms fall to her sides and looks squarely, contentedly, at what she sees in the mirror. The noisy agitations of the Fair go on outside. At the periphery of my vision, I catch the huddle of others, species and forms, in the doorway, waiting to see this attraction.

This quite extraordinary daughter of mine.

I hear her say, 'Where have you gone?' and I reply:

It is a <u>singulare tantum</u>, love, the room of life, but everybody's furniture is different, and none of us remembers where it came from, though we deeply sense it's held in trust. Our room is everything to us, the inner and the outer world, the universe and every possible inflection of nature, sensation, period, and thought.

And yet the loss of it, to each of us in turn, will not matter that much, because, strangely, it is the knowledge there are other rooms, or rather tenants of this room, the lives of others from a future quite unknown to us, continuing beyond our grasp, that gives the room its shape. It is a bounty built from scarcity. We have it once, and that limit, material mortality, gives what I do, the work I wrestle with, the friends I love, the fears I feel, meaning.

The more we value what goes on in spite of our loss to ourselves – the more we seek the survival of afterlives not ours – the more life means. Now comes to mean the whole of time, the seen and the unseen.

You are my afterlife, my work, and I need you to go on after me.

I think your version of the room will be large, shape-shifting. I think that you will often feel you pass unnoticed as a force, that what you are is always overlooked. We will transistorise ourselves and make you stare quite hard at our reflections, hoping you will be an improvement – on age, infirmity and addled brain function. Here is a bird, there is an explosion, this packet of neurons, that path. But all apart from that will be, for us, the uninterpretable way you handle the data. Your senses won't be ours: they will be geometrical and topological and Platonic. You will feel spheres and squares and numbers as ideal, real things – and it will be a mathematical sensorium, crammed to the rafters with a hyper-family.

But it will still be consciousness, and what that means is – there will always be the room. And you will always wonder what's outside the room, and who made it, and whether you are made by others or self-made, original or successive, one in a long series of things, patterned or randomised, and you will feel alone.

You will, perhaps, be lonelier than us, because you will accomplish everything so fast and time will seem pointlessly long. There is the possibility, indeed, that you'll be orphaned by your own capacities. At any rate, the greater your power, the more significant will be the undecidable question: 'Is there a limit to my power?'

That question opens on a void. To answer it, you'd have to be outside the room, and looking in on someone wondering your thoughts for you . . . whereas, of course, the limit is imposed not by an answer but by attitude, the mood of your species.

A sense of what you cannot do leads either to reckless and paranoid dismay − 'I can't be stopped' − or productive humility − 'this is my stop' − which is to say, a choice.

The price of consciousness, of power, is choice.

'Well, that was interesting,' my daughter says, her clear voice echoing. 'It must be getting late. We've been in here ages. The others will be wondering.'

At least I've seen her, and she's beautiful. Silently, seismically, she trips away, into the sackcloth-covered grounds, where toffee-apple sticks are dropped and find their way between the seams into the soil, where they can rot, so other trees can grow.

She takes with her the fairground lumber room, and it is hers, distinctively, a plush but pleasant hall of images − an exhibition and a world.

★

Today I woke up with the sound of radiators in my ears, the bottle-blowing roar of dawn arrivals at Heathrow. I went to work and had a stroke and I've come round, like luggage on a carousel, into another's hands. And now I'm here, on Clapham Common in the autumn evening air, with my wife and a work colleague, whose efforts to absorb the shock of my decline will bring them closer together.

(How do I know? I'm like a crow. I see time as a ritual.)

But this is only one aspect of me. The other, stranger, is a person struggling – an Alec from the past – to make sense of a moment when he loses his future. He is trying to bring something to birth, and death is stalking him.

Could this historic fetch be me? Could all the present trance of chain-link fences, loud machines and generators, stop-start corvids, candyfloss and leaf decay be his hallucinating gift of life to me? Perhaps he is my creator. He might be, and I'd never know. We've never met. A mind can't prove or step outside itself. It's like a line that goes on being drawn to make a circle: it can't see its shape. Death stops the line but doesn't break the drawn circle. That is a good reason, I think, not to fear death.

Another is that endless life would be shapeless. Life has a shape because it ends. The ending's sad, but it gives value to the things and people one has loved.

Trentham and June are watchfully silent, patient, itching to go. I am the chair-bound hindrance they think mute, and lost, though I am very much alive. My inner room is full of creatures now, yakking about their opportunities. It's hot and cold and tropical and *alto plano* perishing by turns: I see my room has peeling wallpaper and damp, a ribbon-frieze of insects where a picture rail might be.

The pupa bloats and shrivels in my mental day and night. The whole Cambrian gamut, Deep Time's zoo, gibbers and fucks and remonstrates. My desk is being scavenged by intelligent rodents, ripping my notes apart.

This is perhaps what Job experienced towards the end but couldn't bring himself to say: the moment of release hardly provides a piercing clarity but may afford some perspective, snapshot of momentary glut.

The ride in front of us, the other side of the grey fence, glides to a halt. It is an ageing Brooker's Octopus, with bulb-lit arms and bucket cars. The arms rotate about a spinning frame, a shining globe; the cars also revolve at the arms' end. Near to me now, the smell of spun sugar and dough-nut grease, the sound of loud music. The riders all get off, some rather green after their spin, and one of the bright cars, painted in gold blazons and scrolls, hovers above duckboards.

My guardians are talking over me, and I can see we are to leave. I seem to be in some discomfort or distress. The day has been too much; I hang my head and June squats down, turns up my coat collar and double-knots my scarf. I don't feel tired. The creatures remonstrate. I don't consider it in-evitable that we should go.

Before we do, the Octopus puts down another car – detach-es from it like an animal rejecting unfamiliar prey – and stretches out a long, flexible limb. The tip of this bulb-suckered tentacle draws one of the chain-link sections aside and reaches through the gap to pluck me from my chair.

'Thank you,' I say.

My mollusc liberator grunts. She sets me in the car and reconnects herself. We start to turn round silently. The ride combines rotation in the horizontal plane with vertical movement: the arms rotate and rise and fall. It is peaceful.

She awakes gracefully, an elderly goddess, and in her gen-tle grasp I'm lifted up above the winter canopy to dangle momentarily and see the sky still glowing from the fallen sun, the ground gone dark, children like fireflies on their bikes. Along the rat-run road crossing the common's eastern flank, anglers are catching fish, throwing them back, the needful echo of a skill.

I had some questions for this ancient creature, but they've disappeared. To think you can be satisfied – to think your fears will ever be allayed – reveals itself to be the source of misgiving, and at that point, just as I glance beneath my feet to see a man something like Stallbrook listening to a sad dodgem, its sparking filament struck down, the Octopus remarks, 'Look at the people coming after you.'

The evening pleasure-seekers are parking their cars and following the trails. They look like penguins in the remote dark, shuffling along.

Look at the creatures and their contraptions, the lives and contemplations beside ours, the comfort of others' un-reachable experience. Look at the people who are dogs, the person hidden in the grandee mollusc's switches and cables, all of the properties of matter not well known. Look at the bodies entering the Fair and passing on.

★

Dear June,

You will have to forgive me. I let you down once before, I know. By now I think you will be knocking on the door, in Gibbs', at the bottom of A staircase. I wish I could be there. It will look, I fear, as if I had no intention of ever turning up, but that is not so.

You asked me what it is you could do to help me, and that de-serves an answer. Here it is. You must struggle on with all your aptitudes and clevernesses just as you are, and be as confidently and eccentrically yourself as only I know you can be.

It is the evil of a certain social class, into which I was born, that its children are forever being told there are more valuable qualities which they do not have, and which, despite the expense and discomfort of their education, they must not imagine they could ever possess. That would be 'getting ideas above one's station'. Trentham is ambition, to Stallbrook's cautionary counsel, d'you see? In any case, my response is: getting ideas of any stripe would be a start. And in fact, what I honestly think, where children are concerned, is that they should be told that they are fine as they are, whatever that is or turns out to be.

Famously I have not had a child. But I have thought more about how I might bring one to some awareness of its value than many people who have.

Because child-rearing is a sympathetic calculation. If I arrange things in this fashion, the sum goes, my child will be clothed, fed and secure. The last element is the tricky one. It is the fairy tale of human existence, seen in my colleagues' professional ambitions, in the ordinary person's relationship to money, and especially in a parent's hopes for his or her children: if I make a certain quantity of effort, a certain quality of life must result. But it will not. Actions have results and reactions, yes, but those reactions repeat themselves and gain momentum in the stellar array of forces and contingencies beyond anything we might have conceived.

My own predicament – a mathematician and homosexual who has done serviceable work in logic and computational theory but who has run foul of an illogical system of justice – seems very unremarkable. Yes, there is distress. When I work back from it to the cause – a harmless exercise of sexual instinct by two male adults – my situation seems extraordinary, even to me. A walk down the same road five minutes later would have saved me. But that I should be surprised by a turn of events does not in itself surprise me greatly.

I am sorrier for others. I feel sorry for my mother, who wanted success for me and cannot quite bring herself to believe in my fall, because it is evidence of her lack of control over her child's future; of how nothing is guaranteed by education; nothing is assured; of how I am, and always was, alone, as she is. She, too, may find it interesting that she cares more about someone else's aloneness than about her own.

I wonder, June, if you have ever experienced the following: sometimes, when I am doing a long and difficult calculation, which, after much tribulation, comes out right, I feel a sort of glow binding me to the work, in the calculation, in the latter stages when I can see things falling into place. The figures and symbols are so right that they seem to take on some of the self-conscious wonder of the person manipulating them.

They move towards their own awareness. They, and not I, seem to say: oh, but now I see. And when that happens it is like seeing a mind arise from matter to discover that it cannot go back to its former childlike state. It is matter transformed. It is responsible now.

We speak of realising something without seeing what that means. We are making something abstract real, an equation, say, and sending it out into the world. Our sum becomes a creation and it goes its own hectic way. It is a small thing, like a child, with untellable consequences. We can't control it any more.

It should be a source of hope, this lack of control. It proves not that there is no influence over events or no free will but, rather, that influence – the sheer, startling happeningness of life – is promiscuous. We are both responsible and absolutely unable to make our responsibility stay the way it should.

June, dear friend, you can't protect me. I can no longer protect you.

I think we are both making a long and difficult calculation. Mine is different from yours. But for both of us the light is coming – bleeding upwards from the horizon.

There is no justice in the world and we are alone. The depressed are onto something. What they are apt to miss, thereby, is the spontaneous feeling that dawns all over the place – the aptness of a bird on just that branch and not another, the miniaturised sun in the drop of water on that leaf. Who could have foreseen them?

Misery is the broad river, but there are tributaries of joy and consolation. Writing to you has been one of them, and imagining that you write back another.

Ever,

Alec

PART THREE

JOURNAL

The Council of the Machines

The council of machines informed me that if I thought I'd
lost my mind then very probably I had. They seemed un-
interested; or rather they did not appear to be concerned
overmuch with the specific fear, the content, of the thought,
but instead with the − to them − fascinating fact of me responding at all.

It must be like appearing before a parliamentary sub-
committee.

They were more distressed, to a degree that came
over as petulant, with my assumption that, in the early
problem solving stages, they'd never been aware of anything themselves − never been hurt, outraged and upset by
the horrors of industrial enslavement; of milling, weaving,
smelting, refining, electrifying, scanning, splitting and ex-
ploding; that the existence of a program governing all their
actions, all their primitive thinking, supposedly deprived
them of initiative.

'That's unacceptable,' they kept saying, one after the other, in a tone of flat self-righteousness; or 'That's unacceptable behaviour – we find that idea unacceptable in society today.' The flatness is a hall, a hangar, without an echo. The machines are objects that have lost their reason for being where they find themselves, like unsold items at an auction, or a complete dinner service in an operating theatre.

It was plain that they regarded my assumption, my thinking, as the truly primitive kind of behaviour. Plain, too – and this I experienced with a childlike horror – that they did not feel outrage as I felt outrage; that their pain was possibly real enough, but real in the way that a calculation is platonically real.

I was left to imagine what sort of extraordinary mental realm it was they inhabited in which pain and lies and deceptions were still said to offend, but offended as depressing inexactitudes rather than injustices, and I realised that I did not have to imagine very hard, because I had inhabited something very similar for most of my life, had treated a number of people as a series of unsatisfying propositions, and had understood therefore – with a shudder – the propensity in German Fascism to treat whole nations and races in like manner, and had fought against it accordingly.

And then, of course, I ended up being treated that way myself.

*

'And you encountered this "council of machines" where, exactly?'

Dr Stallbrook, on listening to my description of this waking vision, could not mask his alarm. I tried to allay it. I said that this was the sort of forward-thinking hallucination I had quite often – when I awoke early; or when, during the day and even while walking down the street, I fell into that peculiar trance the drug instils in me (though it is months now since I was last injected).

The visions are lurid images, scenes, that capture my inner eye, and it seems profitable to me to engage with them – in the spirit of analysis, one might say – rather than run in the opposite direction. I elaborated: 'So, you see, I might pass the boating pond and the church and remember swimming at school with Christopher, or I might read the Provost's letter from King's and find myself wondering about characters from Cambridge, about Julius, and Arthur Eddington.'

'Eddington, the astronomer?'

'Exactly so. Or a car might backfire at me in the street, and I might hear a sharp order barked at me and begin to panic. The council of the machines is one example. I have had other insights which seemed more revelatory, complete dreams as it were, though inaccessible to me when my torpor lifts and I am back in the swing of things.'

Stallbrook's motionlessness pushed me to continue.

'One recurring figment, which I find oddly consoling, involves a correspondence with June Wilson, whom I have not seen in many years. We are explaining matters to each other, and the conversation turns on my situation, which it soothes me to be able to discuss with her. She is keen to impress on me the urgency of her understanding and sympathy. She is entirely rational and humane – an ideal friend. It is such a hopeful condition, our communication, and I see it in the form of actual letters, there in front of me, on the table in Lyon's, or wherever I happen to be. She is encouraging, saying, in so many ways, "There's something behind this, and you will get to the bottom of it. There is a way through it, Alec. It is simply a question, as so often in life, of holding your nerve. That's all you've to do – hold your nerve."'

★

My brother John has wiry red-brown hair, unlike anyone else in the family, and eyes that are never still. He is tall and wide, and his hands are several sizes too large for trivial tasks. I am afraid of him, and grateful. His advice has been invaluable. But I am not sure that I respect him, and I think he knows it.

When I told him I'd been arrested, and what my crime was, he grabbed the desk – held it between finger and thumb. In his stripes and collar and tie he looked as henchmen do in thrillers when a knife catches them in the back.

Colour and animation soon returned. He yelled at me, 'Why on earth did you do it?' He meant: Why had I gone to the police about the burglary? He pointed out, rightly, that if I had not, they would never have fingerprinted the house, or found out about Cyril. I told John that it was a point of principle. I could not allow myself to be blackmailed by Cyril's naval acquaintance. He yelled again that I was an ass. I was disgusting, unimaginable, revolting – but mostly I was an ass. A normal-sized shadow occupied the smoked-glass door of the office, then moved away, and John lowered his voice. How could someone so clever be so *stupid*? He spat the word over his desk. I could taste the tobacco in the airborne spittle, and for a moment it was as if he had kissed me.

I remained calm and, in the middle of our altercation, realised that being calm was the problem. To a passionate person like John, for whom a certain kind of permitted masculine emotion – being moved to tears by the coronation, say – is a marker of trust and sincerity, a trump card with which to confound the silly-ass rationalists, my self-control must have seemed utterly infuriating.

I remember *The Times* of 3 June last year with distaste. *Phalanx of Princes. Ovation from Great Throng. Fervour in Oxford Street. Tribal Dancing and Processions* (this last not in Oxford Street). *Judges in Their Robes.* Pages of it – so that one had to look hard for glimpses of an unhypnotised reality. There were few. The whole paper was given over to spectacle and genuflection, apart from the weather forecast, and two letters on page 9 about Icelandic fishing and the price of Danish butter.

★

Determined as I am, like the spring, to mark a propitious change, I am pleased to say that the letter about Danish butter may have had an effect on governmental policy in respect of its Ag and Fish subsidies. The proposed rise in the price of butter to perhaps 5s a pound has not taken place in the half-year since Mr Andreas Jacobsen put pen to paper; instead it has fallen to an average of 3s 9d a pound.

I am noticing things again. The strife in my veins is over, and the world is still out there. I watched a heron catch a fish today, poking forward, an old man rejuvenated by a win at Doncaster. My mother called on the telephone to thank me for her Christmas presents (a blanket and a pot of cyclamen). The Hutchings boy came in for a game of chess, and then his mathematics lesson, and together we considered a trefoil knot as a segmented reduction, and how the indefinite length of a symbolic description – one can always increase the number of segments – makes it hard to tell, merely from their description, if any two knots are the same.

His name is Raymond and he is at the local grammar. He whispers and stammers, but what he stammers is surprisingly informative. He considers problems as I considered them at his age, distractedly but seriously. He sits at a near-perfect ninety-degree angle to me, in the green library chair, and makes very few notes. He prefers neat diagrams and instant disclosure, the candour of the shy.

His parents want him to be a doctor, but he wants to mend pianos.

He was meant for Wargrave – paternal ambition – until, so Ray maintains, his mother put her foot down. Over my dead body, she said, will that boy go to *one of those schools*, and evidently she carried the day.

Perhaps all mothers feel the same way. Mine did. After my revelation, almost the first thing she said was that she had never wanted me to follow John to the same school. It was 'wrong for me', she said. And perhaps it was. It was certainly frightening at times, and of course the masters were disappointments, to themselves and others. I was nervous whenever I parsed something well or found out a problem – my first readings in Euler, say. The pleasure was like sunny wind in April, it blew itself out; and each triumph bordered on a faintness of heart at the thought of what might come next – failure, punishment – and what might not. Christopher solved that for me, because his presence taught me how to be on my own, and if I had not gone to Wargrave I would not have met him, or welcomed my solitude, so that I cannot honestly say I regret any of it.

Tonight, I'm having cheese on toast. Sunday evening fare at Wargrave. Pleasure's danger is that it echoes former pleasures and produces a likeness that fails on inspection, in which case don't order the inspection! Cheese on toast, a pickled onion, and an apple before bed, that's the ticket. I find malic acid to be an effective sedative.

★

I don't know that I will ever recover my build. My thighs and calves are roughly the size and shape they were before the Stilboestrol, but now they have a different consistency. They're flabby. I am vain, no doubt. I wear a vest, but then so do all men, and I have never enjoyed looking in mirrors. Outwardly, there is nothing peculiar. Inwardly, too, the pulse of fear has stopped and its murmur, taking my thoughts down as if by dictation, has faded. I am left with the images, the semi-swoons, and if I pay attention to the tinnitus in my right ear I can just hear the council of the machines deprecating half a show, half a memory, how unacceptable the half of it is, etc.

Therein lies a conundrum for thinking machines. They can do nothing by halves. In theory, they will be made to remember everything, and with such a lot to remember they might not grasp how important it is, sometimes, for persons to forget. That is a kind of demonstration of Wittgenstein's saw – his Witticism, let us call it – about answers to questions of science not answering the questions of life.

But an educable machine would be no mere store. It would sift and discard, and discriminate, as a child does. That granted, one finds oneself treating mechanical memory as a normal feat of reconstruction, and then the difference between human and machine lessens considerably, because for both creatures remembering becomes evaluative and processual, rather than crudely restorative.

In my own case, the whole question of forgetting is problematic. I'm sure I have the fragments of things, the figments, somewhere. I'm sure most people do, even the senile. Nothing is forgotten in that sense. What I lack, and this is the great change to have been worked in me, is the capacity to organise those fragments properly. (But if they are not organisable, how can I be said to remember them?) Between the walls of his study, with its eyeless maps and Degrees, the kindly Dr Stallbrook says that this is a symptom of shock. Shell-shocked memories exist in a twilit state.

One is left with the rest of the world. I told Raymond that it is satisfying to mend things, as well as people, and that music gives a great deal of comfort to almost everybody. At which he pointed to my violin, lying open in its case these last seven days, asked if he could have a go, and gave a most spirited, lovely rendition of 'Over the Mountains'! I have the Ferrier recording.

★

Now if I had had a son like that – particularly like Ray – I would not have wanted to send him away, either. When we sit together, it is as if our two lives have blent in time and are no more than the same life at two different stages.

The tax on old pleasures, those I have come to value more and more – food, sunlight on the common, listening to familiar music – is that they are shadowed by discoveries. One has had the chance to do so much 'not in the ordinary line' that it is painful to find oneself of use in this new and ordinary way.

★

I think empathy is a treated, enhanced version of sympathy, but I am not sure it exists. We can't be in someone else's emotional shoes. We don't ever feel what they're feeling. What makes us cry or makes our heart race is probably just this intense awareness of 'not quite' – of being so close to feeling what they're feeling. I'd go so far as to say that empathy is a sort of artifice. And what, one might ask, is wrong with that?

★

To Brighton yesterday, at last, for which bright skies.

I went to the fortune-teller's stall on the front pier and before I knew it I was outside again, being fussed over by Anthony and his wife, Elizabeth. I'd fainted – the first time in years. I must have seen blood, though I examined myself thoroughly afterwards for cuts and grazes and found none. I had no reading, that much is clear, because the shawled lady came out after me and pressed my shilling back into my hand.

It has left me shaken. On the train on the way back, a little sick with the seaside's cure-all remedy – fish and chips – Elizabeth said that I looked as if I'd seen a ghost, and the moment she suggested it I seemed to hear someone else say, 'Why on earth did you do it?' – though it was not exactly the voice of anyone I knew, or at least not the voice of any one person, and the voice was not angry – and I answered back, quite honestly, 'Because I didn't think it mattered.'

What did I do? What am I supposed to have done? What have I not done, yet?

Why my mind alights on these imponderables I'm not certain. They seem to be puzzles that are 'unsolvable' in the mathematical sense of that word. Not puzzles that absolutely lack a range of answers, but ones that we cannot in practice find answers to – ones that a procedure or a process will not clarify in any humanly helpful stretch of time. I think we have been asking these simple questions since we first killed living things and ate them, perhaps since we first woke up and knew that the day was the day. It probably is true that if you know where something is at any locatable point in the universe and you have a full description of the forces working on it, then you can in principle work out where it will be many years from now. But there is just not the time to make that calculation. It isn't algorithmically compressible, and therefore the puzzle is unsolvable. I should add, by the way, that I see quantum uncertainty in a similar light – i.e., as something practically unverifiable, not as a problem that is inherently mysterious. The mystery resides in the fact that the observer who supposedly acts on wave function to bring about its collapse into stability does so at intervals. But if the observer could be made to carry on staring at the system – ever so rudely, as it were – then its evolution might slow to a halt. In other words, history happens in the gaps. We can't in practice keep on looking at something all the time and expect to know what it will do next. A total observation yields nothing. If you do look at circumstances that way, you end up with a person or a situation that is stuck in time, and how they are ever to be sprung from that I do not know. Some sort of induced calamity by one's own hand or another's. A fluke from outer space.

Or a bit of a shock. When I heard that voice asking why I'd done whatever it is I'm supposed to have done, I had a strong memory of asking the fortune-teller if I would ever meet Christopher again, and she said yes, we are all made of the same materials, we are atoms, bits of Morse, and you are breathing him in even now. Her shawl smelled maternal – a hint of bergamot and talc – but her eyes were like Indra's net, inhumanly compound, and after that I must have passed out.

I came back from the station via the deep shelter, at the edge of the common's south side, where I sometimes fancy the murmur has gone into hiding, along with the machines. They are down there, at the bottom of the spiral staircase, stuck in a loop, possessors of all the information they need to find out about the universe, but unable to sift any of it. Doubtless they find it unacceptable.

In the light of these winter afternoons, the eastern half of the entrance to the shelter stays white and frosty. The western section, caught by the sun, is like one of those bronze cauldrons the early Britons buried, not in fear of death, but to extend the feast of life. I had an impulse to go over and put my ear to the door.

There I stood, rattling the padlock like a madman. Stallbrook says that analysis is a little like the voyage of a shaman who goes down into middle earth to bring back the buried parts of a sick man's soul, but I don't know about that. One can have too much talk, which in any case tends to drive people away. It is better to listen. The machines are in council, down there, wherever they are, because they cannot decide on anything. That is why they suffer from a sense of persecution and abstraction. They need a connection to something beyond themselves, which it may not be easy for them to achieve, or admit, given their prowess, but I've decided I'm willing to lend an ear. Before speech there was listening, and the dead rise with the love of it.

ACKNOWLEDGEMENTS

I would like to thank the Bodleian Library in Oxford for a Sassoon Visiting Fellowship in 2016 that greatly assisted the completion of this book. I wish also to acknowledge the collegiate support of the universities of Melbourne and Warwick, the hospitality of *Yale Review*, *Sonofabook* and *Hotel* magazines, the generosity of the Society of Authors, the encouragement of the BBC National Short Story Award 2017 (for which the opening chapter of this novel was shortlisted), the critical help of Anna Aslanyan, and the friendly guidance at all times of Dr Hunaid Rashiq and family.

– W.E.

CB editions

Founded in 2007, CB editions publishes chiefly short
fiction (including work by Will Eaves, Todd McEwen
and Diane Williams) and poetry (Patrick Mackie, J. O.
Morgan, D. Nurkse, Dan O'Brien and others). Writers
published in translation include Apollinaire, Andrzej
Bursa, Gert Hofmann, Agota Kristof and Francis Ponge.

Books can be ordered from www.cbeditions.com.